GHOSTS, GULLS AND GERMAN GIRLS

Guy Charles

Grosvenor House
Publishing Limited

The right of Guy Charles to be identified as the author of this
work has been asserted in accordance with Section 78
of the Copyright, Designs and Patents Act 1988

The book cover is copyright to Guy Charles

This book is published by
Grosvenor House Publishing Ltd
Link House
140 The Broadway, Tolworth, Surrey, KT6 7HT.
www.grosvenorhousepublishing.co.uk

This book is a work of fiction and, although some stories are
based on actual events, names and details have been changed,
and the stories do not necessarily accurately reflect the
events as they happened.

A CIP record for this book
is available from the British Library

ISBN 978-1-83975-088-5

Acknowledgements

I would like to thank Helen, Thomas, Mike and Angela for reading the proofs of this book and for making much-needed improvement suggestions.

Contents

Horrid Men..1

Queen Victoria in Difficulty 7

Sex on the Train 10

The Ghost 13

Wilson..18

Going Down a Bomb 24

Blush or Flush?..28

Twenty-Three Tons 32

German Girls 38

Boys and Girls Come Out to Play......................43

The Great Game...47

Realisation 55

Rin Tin Tin...58

Flexibility 62

In the Mood 72

Chinese Whispers 78

Difficult to Accept...84

Artistic Drive..90

The Balcony 94

CONTENTS

Portage...102

St Paul's..109

The Scan 116

Bear..124

Horrid Men

The hotel was very welcoming. Charles and Kathryn received a personal tour of the facilities, shook hands with the owner and received a free welcoming drink by the pool. However, the terms were bed and breakfast, so it was necessary to venture into Old Funchal each evening in search of dinner. As they ambled along on the first evening, they were promptly assailed by numerous café owners, keen to usher them through the door of their various establishments.

'What horrid men,' said Kathryn.

They tore themselves free and eventually had a reasonable meal in a restaurant where the "front man" was a woman and rather more empathetic and less forceful than the norm.

Kathryn and Charles were quick learners and adapted their tactics to looking at menus around 4pm when tramping back from a levada walk, complete with rucksack and boots. "Looking for later" was then more likely to be taken at face value, with "horrid men" consequently giving more explanation of the menus and making less effort to force them over the thresholds there and then.

Various establishments were tried and a favourite found; £10 for three courses, a pleasant and attractive pair of waiters and a characterful piano player with an enormous girth and a propensity to require a ciggy after every six or seven songs of his enormous repertoire. Receipt of a free glass of Madeira while contemplating the bill was a welcome bonus and there were handshakes all round upon leaving.

On their second visit, it started to rain. There were fewer passers-by than normal and Kathryn and Charles were two of only four people in the restaurant. By now, the former "horrid man" out front was becoming admired by the pair for his dauntless, if futile, efforts to guide people in.

'How can they make a living?'

'You have to feel sorry for him, out in that all evening.'

'Look, these four might come in – let's smile as if we're really enjoying it… Oh dear, no good.'

Then, from out of the sodden murk, appeared a North African with something to sell. Passers-by being few, he began to peer through the windows of restaurants. Kathryn stiffened at the prospect of interacting with another "horrid man". Perhaps she was especially sensitive because of an unfortunate experience in the South of France a year earlier. An unemployed Frenchman had decided to force himself on the customers of a restaurant. The fourth time he had placed a supremely tacky bracelet on their table, Charles had knocked it to the floor, producing a vitriolic outburst containing numerous elements of French vocabulary that Kathryn had not learnt at school. In retrospect, Charles considered himself lucky not to have been punched or knifed. He did not wish to have a similar experience with another "horrid man" and avoided eye contact. It was probably the thunderclap that made him look up. The North African proffered his basket. Charles shook his head and the North African smiled, gave him a thumbs-up and trailed off to the next line of cafés.

On the third visit, they were greeted like valued friends. The frontman shook them affably by the hand as they entered and summoned the waiters, who did the same, before ushering them to their "usual" window table. The restaurant was fuller than before and the game of "who can spot the piano player's show tune first" was rendered more difficult by a loud English quartet at the adjoining table. Their booming, plummy voices inferred privilege and money. There seemed to be a connection with journalism, judging from the editorial names being bandied about. All four seemed keener to talk than to listen and this led to friction.

'Martin, do let me finish; I have an important point to make.'

'Whether your point is more important than mine, I very much doubt.'

'Peter, I'd like to contribute a story I've never mentioned before.'

'Originality will make a change anyway, Maisie.'

The conversation, once it did get underway, tended to be political. As Charles became older, his own political opinions had become less acute, as his memory had become vaguer and the limits of his knowledge more apparent. Not so the dauntless four; they knew.

'Martin, in 2003, you said quite explicitly: "I trust Tony Blair and I'm sure he must be doing the right thing with regard to Iraq". That just shows how much store should be set on your opinions.'

'Marjorie, I hardly think that one opinion expressed more than ten years ago should be held against me.'

Suddenly, they were off with the Gulf War. This was perhaps the one topic on which Charles had an opinion. He had a friend who had worked on the *Chilcot Enquiry*, at this time yet to be published. He knew of mounds of evidence received and in the process of being cross-checked. It was surely not possible to know the ins and outs until at least some of this was in the public domain. More conversation floated past...

'Maisie, I am afraid your opinions cannot be expected to carry weight, because they are based on so much less evidence and analysis than my own.'

At this moment, proceedings were interrupted by a tapping at the window. It was the North African. He was demonstrating a variety of the collapsible bowls he kept in his basket.

'What's this fellow up to?' asked Martin.

'Oh look at the bowls; what a clever idea and he has such a sweet black face. I might buy one, you know.'

'You're surely not going out there now, just as the desserts and coffee are finally arriving?'

'Well no,' said Maisie slightly crestfallen, 'But maybe later.'

Fifteen minutes later, the meal was coming to an end.

'Oh look', said Maisie. 'There's the man again' and she made for the door before she could be gainsaid.

The African, his latest attempt at a sale having failed, was loping along and, as Maisie scuttled through the door, it was clear that she might not have the pace to catch him or the confidence to call out. Charles caught the African's eye, glanced towards Maisie and gave a slight nod. It was amazing how much non-verbal information could be conveyed in a quarter of a second. The African spun on his heel and retraced his steps. However, the sale was by no means a foregone conclusion. Maisie found it necessary to scrutinise every collapsible bowl in his basket. Did she want one or not? If so, what would be the best size?' Suddenly, another couple appeared. Seeing the wares displayed to best advantage, they became interested too. Kathryn and Charles looked on, fascinated. Would he make two sales, one sale or none at all? Suddenly, Martin had had enough. He burst through the door.

'For goodness sake, Maisie, you don't want any of this trash. Send him on his way and let's get back to the hotel.'

'I can't bear it, Charles,' whispered Kathryn. 'If neither of them buy one, you'll have to.'

However Martin's intervention had expedited Maisie's decision-making.

'I'll have that one,' she said, pointing to a biggish example.

'Completely ridiculous,' said Martin. 'What on earth do you think you'll do with it?'

However, the money was safely handed over and the bowl changed hands. Encouraged by this, the other couple also took the plunge and bought, though a rather smaller specimen.

Maisie and Martin re-entered the café and the four took their leave, noisily debating whether that steak really was rump and supposing they had better leave some sort of tip, though the waiters had been very slow fetching the starters and the brandy had been by no means the best.

In the meantime, the African packed up his remaining wares and set off down the street, not neglecting to pause briefly at the window to smile at Charles and give him a covert thumbs-up.

Queen Victoria in Difficulty

A tiger was abroad in the streets of the town. Rees first encountered it in an alcove at the market. There it was, astride an unfortunate woman dressed in Victorian costume and wearing a crown.

A nearby stallholder grinned and nodded at a red button on the wall, which Rees promptly pressed. The tiger chomped its jaws and roared, while the royal personage drummed her heels and rolled her eyes. After a repeat performance, Rees sighted further information on the wall opposite.

The exhibit was intended to demonstrate how a resurgent India had turned the tables on the British Raj, here depicted by a desperate Queen Victoria being consumed by a tiger.

Rees was overwhelmed by the vision, time and determination that had gone into the creation. And how did one negotiate such a project with one's partner, he wondered? Rees could envisage his own wife's reaction should he himself have suddenly said, 'I thought I'd make a moving exhibit of Queen Victoria being eaten by a tiger, dear.' Though some wives, he surmised, might embrace the project, perhaps enthusiastically giving a hand with the papier mâché. Others, he supposed, after the first wave of shock or admiration, might quietly enjoy the seclusion implicit in their spouse's visit to the garage to get Queen Victoria's eyeballs just right. In any event the determination and energy required to see the project through could only be admired.

A couple of months later, Rees was browsing in a pop up shop depicting the work of local artists when he heard a familiar roar emanating from a corner and there, sure enough, was the unfortunate Queen Victoria being consumed by the tiger for perhaps the five thousandth time. Rees could not resist giving the button a few more presses himself.

Once again, he admired the effort that had gone into the creation. Surely, though, the intention had not been to create a kind of "Flying Dutchman" exhibit, doomed to wander the shopping centres of the town forever? This time, there was a little more accompanying information, which Rees was able to amplify through conversation with two of the volunteers who ran the shop.

Apparently it had been hoped that the exhibit would be displayed nearby in a National Trust property. However, ultimately it had been rejected, because, it was thought, of its anti-royalist sentiments. And certainly a National Trust property Rees had visited recently had seemed to wish to downplay its early owners' association with India in favour of stressing the much less controversial re-siting of a girls' school, as part of the evacuation procedures of the Second World War. No, clearly there they wouldn't want feelings stirred by a carnivore, specialising in the consumption of royalty, and this might well be the general National Trust view.

So it appeared that the tiger was condemned to haunt local shopping malls for as long as its vocal cords lasted. It would be interesting, thought Rees, to see how it would be received if it could somehow make the long trip to India. However, that didn't seem very likely and off he went to give the button a final press.

Sex on the Train

Rees was on the slow train to the Welsh coast and slowly giving way to his inner fur seal. Perhaps the estuary through which they were passing, iconic fur seal habitat, or else last night's documentary had kick-started the partial metamorphosis.

If seal philosophy became predominant in human nature, Rees realised that, with the approach of the breeding season, he would have to begin by barging the other males out of the carriage. Then he would have to mate with the females, perhaps several times. Both prospects were daunting to a middle-aged male.

In a way, he was fortunate regarding the barging. This was not a train full of football supporters, where opposition could be expected to be substantial and he might well find himself suddenly sprawled upon the platform. There was a youngish man dozing over there. Clearly, the element of surprise would be vital in his case. Then there was the trio of elderly walkers. Rees felt reasonably confident about taking them on individually. The problem would be if they combined against him. His mind drifted back to the documentary. No, as far as he could recollect, seals tended to act individually in their confrontations. Probably

strategically the best option was to await the outcome of the tussles between the trio of walkers, the
businessman engrossed in his laptop and that bald
bloke reading his paper. Then he would take on the
winner.

Assuming he triumphed, that left the sex. The
beach overlord seals had put themselves about with
regard to any female present. Was it necessary to be
quite so indiscriminate? Also, there was no detail in
the documentary about the behaviour of older
females. Perhaps they did not return to the beach
at all? Might, then, that pair of older women just
get off? This would lessen the load for a male, who
was, after all, past his prime. However, unless the
process of sealisation was very well established,
Rees was uncomfortably aware that, nonetheless,
the procedure would take a very considerable time.
And the female seals on the beach had not seemed
to have concerned themselves very much about
snacks and refreshments. Unless seal nature became
almost totally dominant with regard to the females
on the train, Rees very much doubted whether the
same philosophy would pertain. Refreshments
would be demanded during the considerable down-
time. Coffee and cake would be wanted at regular
intervals and whole meals required if nights in
the sidings were needed. Rees seriously doubted
whether the comestibles in the adjoining dining car
were sufficient for the purpose.

Also, the female seals on the beach had seemed
placidly accepting of the male merely flopping on
top of them from time to time and getting it over
with . Rees was uncomfortably aware that, unless

philosophical metamorphosis was virtually complete, the modern female was likely to expect considerably more, particularly, he thought, that young woman at the end of the carriage with the tattoos and piercings. It was all going to be very difficult and daunting.

Fortunately, the approach of his station jolted Rees back into a more human frame of mind and it was with more than usual relief and alacrity that he disembarked onto the platform.

The Ghost

It seems funny to be packing it in after all these years. I must have marked 120,000 books and then there's been all those curricular changes... The thing is, I've enjoyed it mostly. I can't help being interested in them and well, liking most of them. That's more than half the battle in my view. They seem to be able to tell if you're interested and want them to do well and to appreciate it, often enough. Everything's a lot easier then.

Anyway, that's all beside the point, isn't it? Ghosts; that's what all this is about. I heard them talking about ghosts the other day. Some new film or other, I expect; lots of blood and violence probably. Well, I thought I saw a ghost once, or heard one anyway. But now I'm not too sure. I'll tell you about it. See what you think.

It was a long time ago. I'd only been teaching about five years. The children I taught then were a bit special. Not unintelligent, you understand, but well, unusual. One or two couldn't talk very well. Most had some problems with reading, but underneath they were as bright as you and me. Then there was Kelvin. Kelvin wasn't like the others. He could talk – too well sometimes and he was the best reader in the class. But he had some funny ideas. He hated being black. One day, he'd tried to paint himself white. Another time, he sat in the changing rooms crying, because he hadn't been able to pick a brick off the bottom of the swimming pool. He reckoned it was because he was black. It didn't matter to him that only two out of the other twenty had managed it. It took me nearly half an hour to talk him around and get his clothes back on. Nowadays, maybe he'd get counselling of some sort; he'd just got me.

Every year, I took the class away for a week. Sometimes we camped, but this particular year we stayed in a youth hostel. It was great, with lots of hills and fields behind. In the evening, half of them could just go out and play around, while we helped the rest get the dinner ready. The only problem was an old quarry with a two-hundred-foot drop. But that was half a mile away and fenced off with three-foot-high metal railings. I just told them to stay close by and it was no problem.

The third day, we went off in the bus to visit this country house. It was about five miles by road and two miles if you walked across the common. We split into groups and had a good look around. There was plenty to see and they were full of questions. One of Henry VIII's wives had lived there; the one who had "survived". Then there were the Samurai warriors and, of course, the jewels. I'd certainly needed to be on top form with my explanations. Anyway, at last we got to the final room. As we were looking at the suits of armour, Paul asked me how they used to go to the toilet. While I was wondering myself, I heard Kelvin talking to one of the attendants. He was looking at one of the pictures on the wall. The attendant was explaining that it illustrated an old Bible story. A man had fallen off a tower and, rather than have him die, God had sent angels to catch him before he hit the ground. I could see why it had grabbed Kelvin's attention. It was certainly eye-catching, with all those golden wings and halos and the poor chap being caught just in the nick of time. I can't remember what I said to Paul now, but soon it was time to gather everyone together for the trip back.

I'd decided to get them to walk, while one of the other staff drove the minibus back. Now you and I know that two miles is hardly any distance at all, but to hear the moans you'd have thought I'd suggested walking to the South Pole. That was part of the problem with most of them; they'd no confidence – they didn't think they could do anything they weren't used to. In the end, I won them over and off we went. Everything was fine for about a mile, but then Paul and Kelvin sat down and said they wouldn't carry on. I pointed out that there was no way back except walking and it was quicker to go forward than back, but this had no effect. In the end, I said the rest of us were carrying on and, in half an hour, we'd be having our tea. I wasn't going to drag them along. So it was up to them. They sat there sulking, so off we went. I knew they'd follow in the end. What other choice did they have?

Sure enough, in twenty minutes, we were back at the hostel. We soon got our boots off and the kettle on. The van driver noticed Paul and Kelvin weren't there. I could tell she was worried and anxious when I explained. So was I, but I wasn't going to show it in front of the rest. I kept peering out of the window and thankfully, in a few minutes, I spotted Paul. I wasn't very pleased and I told him he'd better get his boots off fast if he wanted his tea. Then I asked where Kelvin was. He said he didn't know. He'd got tired of waiting and left Kelvin on his own.

Serves him right, I thought grumpily as I went back to my room to get the matches for the stove. Then I heard the voice as plain as day, quiet but insistent: '*Go and find him.*' I looked around to see who it was. Nobody was there. I even looked behind the door to see if anyone was fooling around. Nobody was there. I went back to my coat for the matches. Then there it was again: '*Bring him home.*'

Well, I don't mind telling you I was feeling a bit shaken. Was I hearing things or what? Anyway, I'd calmed down a bit by now, so I decided I'd better go.

I couldn't find him at first. I walked straight back to where we'd left him; no sign. I circled around for a bit and at last I caught sight of him. He was over by the disused quarry. I was just about to yell over and ask him what on earth he thought he was doing when something stopped me. He'd climbed the metal fence and was perched right on the edge of the two-hundred-foot drop.

'Just a minute, Kelvin,' I said calmly and walked over. 'What are you doing?' I asked quietly.

'Well, I was just wondering, sir, if I threw myself off here, do you think God would send some angels to catch me?'

I went cold all over.

'No, Kelvin,' I said, 'I don't think He would.'

'Does he only save white people?' he asked with a scowl.

I'd have laughed if it hadn't been so serious.

'No,' I said. 'Think of the man in the picture; he wasn't white, was he?' I could tell I'd struck the right note by Kelvin's thoughtful look and the clearing of his brow.

'It's just that I don't think nowadays God acts quite like he seemed to in those old Bible stories. Promise me you won't try anything like that, Kelvin.'

'Okay sir,' said Kelvin, coming over to join me. 'Will I be back in time for my tea?'

And that's all there is to tell; or nearly all. I hadn't thought about it for ages. But with retirement approaching you can't help reminiscing and I happened to mention it last week to that newly qualified teacher, the RE specialist. Anyway, after I'd finished, I said, 'Fancy Kelvin thinking God would do something to save him. Daft, wasn't he?'

'Was he?' was all she said.

It got me thinking, though. I don't think I know what to make of it all. What do you think?

Wilson

The mores of the educational system in which Rees worked were vastly different from those when he attended school himself.

There had been forty-four children in his primary class, staffed only by a teacher. It would be rare today to find a state schoolboy educated in isolation from girls between the ages of seven and eighteen. It would be inconceivable for a primary year group to rate each other on their boxing skills and arrange regular fights in the playground to adjust rankings, with no interference from staff. The past is another country indeed.

And in this country, Rees moved to grammar school, a place where staff beat pupils for failing to stand if a senior master or a woman entered the room and where sixth formers were permitted to smoke in their common room. Staff referred to pupils by their surnames, boys with common ones having numbers attached, there being in Rees's form an unfortunate boy known as Smith 13.

Rees was not a high-status individual with his peers as he moved through school. He kept himself in the upper half of the top set by working extremely hard, an attribute not particularly admired by less diligent classmates. Rees was physically unimposing, being at one time the smallest boy in his year. He neither spoke of nor demonstrated any prowess with girls. In this other country, Rees's family did not obtain a record player until he was seventeen and a transistor radio did not prove a firm enough foundation for Rees to be able to speak with any authority on modern trends in music. Fortunately, Rees did have an important redeeming feature; he was interested in sport and quite good at it. As with everything else, sport was hierarchical. Alpha males played rugby, beta males played hockey and a small band regarded as mad, but not soft, did cross-country. After some years of failing at these sports, the hoi polloi (the more able pupils studied Ancient Greek) were permitted to take up sports such as badminton or table tennis, though obviously forfeiting any rights to esteem from the alphas and betas.

Rees had been watching rugby since the age of six and knew more about it than the rest of his football-raised year. He was not big, not fast and his kicking was limited. However, he could see gaps and space and had a knack of putting teammates or even occasionally himself, into these and so he made the year group team. With circuit training on Monday lunchtimes, practice all Wednesday after-noon and matches on Saturday, the school was generally successful. It defeated most schools with the exception of the generally famous (Manchester Grammar School) or those firmly established in rugby league heartlands (Normanton).

Rees himself had a varied attitude to the game. What could be better than creating the winning try on a sunny autumnal morning? What worse than having to drop on the ball again behind a beaten pack on a wet blustery February afternoon? Particular purgatories were endured on Wednesday afternoons during years seven and nine, for two year groups trained together and the year group above Rees was freakishly good, going through several seasons unbeaten, whatever the opposition. It had a mighty pack and two flankers, Mick Norman and Pete Rowley, who could more or less do as they pleased with Rees, like two cats with a mouse, as he stumbled about behind his retreating pack. Fortunately, after a couple of demonstrations of their prowess, though not exactly gentle, they did not set out to maim. Obviously, though, these were not sessions for Rees to relish.

Given the legendary toughness of the older squad, it might be thought that here would be rivalry for the accolade of "hardest man". But no, this was unanimously agreed to be Jonny Wilson, the number eight. Wilson did not generally deign to exert his fearsome powers on lesser mortals a year younger at practice, but would reserve them for when "push came to shove", so to speak, in some ferocious encounter against a top team.

When Rees entered his final year, The Immortals had left, except for one. It appeared that Wilson had not done as required in his exams and had had to stay on. Would he be turning out in the first team with Rees and his peers? No, he made no appearances on any rugby pitch at all. His legendary status was such that enquiries could not be made,

'What the fuck's it got to do with you?', being one anticipated reply.

Rees was, therefore, astonished to find himself tapped on the shoulder by Wilson mid-season. Fighting down a ridiculous desire "to deny everything", Rees asked if he could be of help.

'You're Rees, aren't you, and picking the team for Stokesay versus Caxton; well, I'll be playing.'

It is traditional on these types of occasions to make referral to lack of attendance at training, limited commitment over the season, necessity to earn your place and so forth. Rees encapsulated all this in his response: 'Okay.'

Wilson then went on. 'I think you might be of some use to me, but what about these other fuckers? Can any of the bastards actually fucking play?'

Something of a debrief then followed in which the strengths and (mainly) weaknesses of the individuals concerned were explained. Then, daringly, Rees ventured a question. 'Er, if you don't mind me asking, Wilson, why have you decided to play in this house match and not the rest of the season?'

'My mates have left, haven't they? It was them I played for, not the fucking school, but these Caxton cunts have been yakking on at me about how they'll win the house trophy and how Stokesay are crap, so I thought I'd show them a thing or two. Get the rest of them there ten minutes early.' With that, he was gone.

Caxton were indeed firm favourites for the trophy, the bulk of them being first team players, particularly the backs from fly half onwards. Even with the mighty Jonny Wilson, it was difficult to envisage a Stokesay victory.

So dawned the day of the 11-a-side (six forwards, five backs) house match and with it Wilson's legendary team talk.

'Me and my mate, Pete Rees, are intent on beating these Caxton cunts today and you bastards are going to help us. You, I hear you've never made a tackle in your life (*a slight exaggeration*). Well, you start today. Otherwise, you'll have me to answer to. You, I hear you're fucking fast. If they kick it downfield, get yourself down there, pick it up and stay on your feet till we get there. Understand? (*nods*). This is how it's going to work. I'll be pro-pping and I pity the poor cunt who's up against me (*so did Rees*). We'll win all of our ball and they'll win not much of theirs. As soon as it comes out, Pete will pick it up, get as far as he can, then slip it to me. I'll make some yards and it'll be another scrum to us and so on. He's never going to pass the ball to you backs 'cos we can't afford any slip ups. Understand? (*collective nods*). And if you do ever get the ball, no kicking; their backs are never to have the ball and we can't control the lineouts like the scrums. Now let's go and fucking beat the cunts.'

Fortunately, at kick-off, Rees managed to kick the ball ten and a half yards, as instructed, and the unfortunate Caxton recipient was shunted several yards downfield by a rampaging Wilson before spilling the ball for a Stokesay scrum. Rees found it quite difficult to stick to the Wilson game plan and not throw out a single pass to his strangely uncomplaining back line. However, fear for his life and the kudos of being referred to as "my mate, Pete" helped him stick to the tactics. Twenty minute halves helped with the Wilson stamina and twice he successfully crossed the line amidst a jumble of bodies. Caxton managed a breakaway try late on, but too little, too late and Stokesay were victorious.

Wilson eyed the post-mortem of his defeated rivals and encapsulated his views by a spit on the grass. Then, with a "Well done" to the rank and file and an appreciative nod to Rees, he went on his way, his point having been proved to his satisfaction.

Some two years later, Rees was walking down the street when he was accosted. 'Pete Rees, isn't it? You helped me beat those Caxton cunts. A fucking student, I expect?' On receiving a reply in the affirmative, he replied, 'Well, I'm in the army. It's a fucking great life for me – come on, I'll buy you a pint; you've no fucking money I expect.' Common ground between the two was limited to approximately the time it took to sup the pint, but Rees was pleasantly touched by the gesture.

Going Down a Bomb

Most professions are hierarchical and so it is with bomb disposal men. The most highly trained and experienced bravely strive to prevent catastrophe against devious and calculating opponents and their improvised explosive devices. This, however, is not a story focusing on incredible bravery, for, as we shall see, not all bomb makers are determined and cunning men and it is with some of these that the more inexperienced officers may initially become involved.

Tommy Anderson had lived in Glasgow most of his life, with the exceptions being time he had spent in prisons outside the immediate Glasgow area. His source of income was neither large nor known. Indeed, it was a surprise to see him with money at all, given his limited enthusiasm for work and a similar reluctance on the part of employers to offer him any. There was speculation that his income arose from the sale of certain illicit substances, the content of which was not always clear even to him. However he was certainly happy to sample his doubtful wares, from time to time, when trade was slow. His income seemed sufficient, though, to pay the rent on a small insalubrious flat and to allow him to visit The Garscube Bar most lunchtimes.

A key component of the lunchtime visits was generally fruitless attempts to liaise with women. Even those involving monetary inducements were generally doomed to failure, much to the amusement of the regular clientele. However, one particular September afternoon, Cupid must have been paying one of his rare visits to Central Glasgow, because, to the astonishment of the regulars, Tommy succeeded. A better writer would provide the dialogue that sparked the success, but Tommy's accent was so ferociously broad that few could understand or replicate it outside the immediate area. Whatever was said was evidently both understood and persuasive, for Tommy left the pub with the woman on his arm.

Arriving at the flat, Tommy was able to provide some cans of lager to mellow the mood, but still found progress slower than he had hoped; time, then, to impress. The gist of the conversation was as follows.

'Let me show you something,' he said and guided the woman into the kitchen, where he proudly gestured to an object on top of the fridge. This had the appearance of a huge ceramic earthenware pot, filled with powder and with a long string drooping from the top.

'What is it?' she asked.

'It's my bomb. Isn't she a beauty?' Tommy answered proudly.

There are a number of crass opening sexual strategies favoured by the less sophisticated male, involving highly personal, if appreciative, remarks, suggestions for direct action or even crude gestures and whistles. None are renowned for their success, but the lesser used "look at my bomb" gambit tends to be an even more spectacular failure. The woman affected to need the toilet, tiptoed through the front door and bolted to the nearest police station.

A bemused Anderson promptly witnessed the arrival of a flashing lights police car and, shortly afterwards, an impressive bomb disposal truck.

Anderson's conversation with the police inspector was both profane and incoherent and a psychiatrist was sent for while the captain and his sergeant addressed "the device".

'Not our most complex job.' The captain grinned, having pulled out the fuse. 'As far as I can tell, it's just various sorts of firework powder compressed into a pot with a fuse rammed in.'

There were procedures to be followed, however. Photos needed to be taken and descriptions written, though the possibility that Anderson had come under the thrall of a master bomb maker who was even now exhorting others to construct devices of similar cunning appeared vanishingly small.

The captain was, therefore, still present when the psychiatrist emerged to give his verdict.

'Though my report regrettably may be more long-winded, my preliminary conclusion is that he is "completely crackers", the probable cause being brain fry from prolonged drug and alcohol abuse. However, were a second opinion to consider him "absolutely barmy", I probably wouldn't argue.

'With regard to the bomb, it appears that his mother died last year, while he was detained at Her

Majesty's pleasure, and he was unable to pay his last respects in a manner he considered appropriate. He made the bomb with the intention of setting it off in the cemetery on the anniversary of her death as a spectacular and fitting tribute to the anniversary of her passing. He's been having second thoughts recently, though. It seems there's a family down the street that's been "disrespecting" him. If he could come by a few ball bearings, he was thinking of adding them to the mix and setting it off in their garden.'

'It sounds as though he could have done some real damage then,' said the more senior policeman. 'We'll take him down to the station and charge him.'

It appeared that Tommy Anderson would not be frequenting The Garscube for some time to come.

Blush or Flush?

There has been considerable psychological research on seat selection. In a waiting room, people will not generally sit next to another person if there are a lot of vacant seats. Both males and females tend to prefer to sit next to a female if obliged to sit next to another person. On trains, people use "baggage strategies" to try to maximise body space.

A problem with modern research is that it tends to deal with relatively civilised situations. Information regarding more basic environments generally has to be obtained anecdotally.

'Toilets,' said The Ancient, 'Are a much neglected topic of conversation.'

His dinner companions rose like startled pheasants from a copse, one to clear the table, one to put food remnants in a bin and a third to wipe the mats, though all feared they were merely postponing the inevitable.

'The worst toilets,' continued The Ancient over coffee, 'Were on troop ships. They were arranged in inward-facing parallel lines, without cubicles; not only could you find yourself with a near neighbour either side, but eyeball to eyeball with the fellow opposite; disconcerting, to say the least. The more fastidious would try to go at night, though, of course, nature did not always allow this. Some rudimentary attempts at privacy could have been made relatively easily, but this was never done; I don't really know why. Perhaps it was an attempt to brutalise.'

The Ancient ruminated on.

'When I was in the Western Desert,' he said, 'There was a man in the next platoon who was widely disliked.'

Has he lost his train of thought? wondered the listeners, hoping that this might indeed be the case.

'I am not certain why,' he went on. 'I do know that he did not smoke and would always try to trade his cigarettes at above the usual rate and that he could not be relied upon to cover another's mistake and tended to indulge in triumphant jeering if a sergeant found fault with a member of his or an adjoining platoon. His platoon rarely spoke to him directly and referred to him in conversation with each other as "The Blister" owing to his continuing propensity to irritate and annoy.

After one particularly troublesome week, one of the more ebullient members of the platoon decided that what The Blister required, was a scorpion in his boot. A suitable specimen was procured and the deed done. The scorpion did not actually sting him, mainly because The Blister trod on it first. However, his reaction was regarded as hilarious by the perpetrator and the rest of the platoon. The Blister, however, took a different view. True, no harm had actually come from it, but this was down to luck and his own alertness. To him, it was the thought that counted and he determined on revenge.'

'The designer of the camp toileting arrangements,' went on The Ancient, 'Had been of an altogether more imaginative cast of mind than his counterpart with regard to the troopship. The facilities were known as "The Christmas Cake" and were circular in design with outward-facing holes set judiciously along the rim. There was even a head-high, two-foot-wide partition between each hole. Each occupant could, therefore, gaze ahead, communing with the desert and fain to be oblivious to the grunter next door. Visiting "The Christmas Cake" could be quite a communal activity. If one of the more basic elements announced his intention to pay a visit, then two or three of his more sociable companions might decide to do the same.

It was this unusual form of camaraderie that allowed The Blister to plan his revenge. Having purloined some fuel oil from the vehicle compound, he crept out just before dawn and poured it down several holes, soaking the considerable pile of paper and detritus in the pit below. After this, it was merely a question of waiting for the communal post-breakfast trip from the most "deserving" members of his platoon. Feigning a visit himself, it was the work of a moment to set a piece of toilet paper alight, drop it on the fuel-soaked contents below and beat a hasty retreat. The results were indubitably spectacular.

I do not know what became of The Blister. Events moved quickly. I do not even know if it could be proved that he was the perpetrator. He was, however, promptly and wisely transferred to another unit, to spare him the wrath of his victims. So let us be glad,' finished The Ancient, 'For civilisation and flushing toilets.'

A sentiment with which his listeners found it hard to disagree.

Twenty-Three Tons

Rees found himself driving over "his bridge" and his mind drifted back forty years. As a student, Rees had been keen to earn money over the summer. He had visited the employment exchange and, with almost unbelievable luck, had been informed that temporary labourers were required to bring a construction project back onto schedule. The pay was surprisingly generous.

So, a day later, he found himself standing on a partly built bypass, which stopped abruptly on the bank of the River Ouse. Two other students were also present. One, Richard, seemed worryingly effete for this kind of work and the other, Ben, seemed as though he didn't really want to be there at all.

'So,' finished Dave, a manager in charge of several miles of construction, 'I'll leave you in the capable hands of Kev here.' And so saying, he promptly drove off.

Over the next few days, it transpired that the project was behind for a reason. A caucus among the workforce resented Capable Kev, who had been brought in above them when the previous foreman had left. They felt they knew more about the specific project and the work in general than he did and would only do precisely what they were told and would offer no constructive suggestions. They resented the incorporation of additional workers and, very likely, students in general.

Rees knew enough to try to keep his head below the parapet, unlike Richard. The trio were interrogated by the workforce in the manner of barracudas sensing blood.

'What's your names?'

'My name's Richard.'

'Yes, you look a right Dick.'

'Actually, I prefer Richard.'

'Gazza, what do you reckon? Have we got a Richard or a Dick?'

'He's definitely a Dick. In fact I've never seen anybody more of a Dick'.

'So you see, we all think you're a Dick. And what do you study, Dick?'

'Sociology actually.'

'Socifuckingology; what the fuck's that?'

Rees regarded himself as exceedingly fortunate that his own name and subject (chemistry) were merely greeted with all-purpose disapproving grunts.

In his circle, Rees, as a rugby playing scrum-half, was regarded as fairly fit at this time. He was not, however, what was termed "hard". Hard men could work for hours at physically demanding tasks; they could also fight. Rees was uncomfortably aware that, if it came to physical confrontation, he could be taken to the cleaners by almost any member of the workforce. He found working for ten hours a day, even on legitimate tasks, exhausting and was astonished by his craving for beer in the evenings.

It would be ridiculous to say that Rees became accepted by the men. He was pleased, however, to be spared the epithet "yercunt", as in 'Come here yercunt', or 'Pick that up yercunt' or 'Dick, yercunt, take that over to Mike.' "Dick, yercunt", was a particular favourite of the workforce, both reinforcing the pecking order and amusing them by the juxtaposition of the words involved.

Although Rees would have liked to believe that personality and work rate had contributed to greater acceptance, he was aware that an important influential factor was Black Joe. Black Joe was the most imposing physical specimen Rees had ever seen. There was quite a lot of overt racial prejudice around at that time. However, from a combination of genuine respect and fear that he might take umbrage, none was ever directed at Black Joe. For reasons that were never clear to Rees, Black Joe took something of a shine to him. From time to time, Black Joe would be asked to undertake difficult tasks requiring almost Herculean strength.

'Yes,' Joe would reply, 'But I shall require this young man to help me.'

Though this was manifestly untrue, Capable Kev had little choice but to comply and so Rees would spend a welcome half an hour merely passing Joe tools, a welcome respite from the usual hard graft. During this time, Joe would explain some of the complexities of his unravelling domestic life or his financial troubles, partly arising from a tremendous backlog of unpaid motoring fines and partly from a limited appreciation of the consequences of high interest rates on loans. Rees would occasionally make tentative suggestions and be greeted with:

'Yes, young man, but I just don't seem able to do that.' or

'Young man, I am pleased to see that you have more sense than to turn into a man like me.'

One Friday Capable Kev told the students they were to report for three hours work on Saturday morning. They would be paid time and a half, an astronomical sum to Rees. During the course of the morning, Rees was able to infer that Kev had been placed on a warning owing to continued slow progress. He had, therefore, decided to take matters into his own hands. The workforce had been singularly unhelpful about the best way of putting a considerable amount of steel cable through ducting and this is what Kev intended to attempt with the help of the students.

The first cable went well enough, the students taking it in turns to pull on a giant hand winch to pull through a lead line and then the attached cable. Work on the second cable came to a halt.

'Put some fucking back into it!' bellowed Capable Kev, in his customary constructive way.

Rees was the student who could put most "back into it", but he could not get the cable to budge. Capable Kev thrust him aside impatiently and began himself. As sweat poured off him, the cable began to inch through, but nobody liked the look of the situation and investigations began. The cable had snagged the metal ducting, which was now all concertinaed and torn and would need replacing.

'Well, lads,' said Capable Kev, 'That's the last you'll be seeing of me.' Then he went off to collect his cards.

On Monday, the situation was more poisonous and chaotic than usual. There was now not even a nominal foreman. Also, Black Joe had been temporarily assigned to a different gang for a few days. A lorry chose this moment to arrive with twenty-three tons of cement.

'Where do you want this, lads? Over here?' The driver pointed to a spot adjacent to the concrete mixers.

'No, over here,' replied someone, pointing to a spot some forty metres away

'Are you sure, 'cos–...?'

'Just do as you're fucking told.'

So, with a shrug, the driver did as he was bid and, having presented his docket, left.

'Now, you three, shift those fucking bags over here.'

'But there's four hundred and sixty of them,' said Richard, 'And you could have had them put there in the first place...It's ridiculous.'

'Just fucking get on with it.'

Rees wasn't at all sure he was going to be able to move his share of the four hundred and sixty bags, let alone, as seemed likely, some extras. However, fifteen minutes later, he was saved by the arrival of Dave.

'What's this? The driver's unloaded them in the wrong place; you should have told him... We'd better all get stuck in or we'll be here all day.'

Richard and Ben did not appear again after this, but actually the worst was over. The next day, a specialist team arrived having just "sorted out some difficulties on an oil rig". They were utterly professional, knowledgeable men who spoke as one. They were even able to get the recalcitrant workforce to work effectively.

Within a few weeks, the bridge was completed on schedule and it was time for Rees to leave. Much to his surprise, as Dave was driving him to the office, he said, 'I'm looking for an assistant; you don't happen to fancy it, do you?'

Rees was speechless and Dave went on, 'Oh don't worry about that lot down there. After the trouble-shooters have been, there's always an action plan. They don't know it yet, but they're getting their cards on Monday.'

'Not Black Joe?'

'Oh no, not him, but most of the rest.'

Nonetheless, Rees politely declined.

German Girls

The German winter of 1945/6 was bitterly cold. The soldiers of the British Army, who had fought their way to Berlin, were being gradually demobbed, to be replaced by younger recruits. The army hierarchy did its best to exert control and discipline. Contact between soldiers and civilian women was officially forbidden, but in truth was common, particularly given that the desperate civilian population would offer almost anything for cigarettes, now the de facto currency. Arms were officially to be borne only on duty, but many of the returning soldiers had acquired sidearms during their adventures, either as souvenirs or as precautionary off-duty protection in a difficult environment. Feeling that the police in Britain may not have the requisite sporting attitude, many veterans offloaded their unofficial weaponry onto new arrivals for a nominal sum.

So it was that eighteen-year-old Leonard Lawrence, relatively inexperienced in affairs of the heart and, for that matter, the loins, found himself encamped on the edge of the Black Forest with a ready supply of cigarettes, a pistol and a German girlfriend, Maria.

Recalling events some seventy years on, Leonard could not remember how he had met Maria. He did recollect, however, that one of the features of the family cottage was an enormous wood-burning stove with a ready supply of fuel from the forest. This provided a welcome respite from the literally freezing conditions prevailing in the barracks.

Leonard's relationship with Maria was complicated by the family situation. Maria herself was somewhat older and was, in fact, married to a German soldier missing on the Russian front. Though presumed dead, there was obvious potential for awkwardness should he suddenly materialise. The other inhabitants of the cottage were Maria's parents, a young man who had lost his leg on the Russian front and his wife.

Perhaps in the circumstances it was surprising that there was sufficient overall cordiality for the visits to continue, but the twin attractions of the stove and Maria were a sufficient lure for Leonard, so the visits carried on, with ultimately an invitation for Christmas.

Leonard accepted and, knowing that festive foodstuffs were likely to be in short supply, he made a particular effort to contribute something practical to the festivities. He wrote home to his mother to ask for coffee, a commodity rare enough in post-war Britain and unheard of in the Germany of that time. To his delighted surprise, a parcel containing the inestimable delicacy duly arrived and, on Christmas Day, armed with this and a bumper carton of cigarettes in his overcoat pocket, he made his way, unhindered, to the cottage.

The comestibles were of a higher standard than might have been expected. The woods had yielded fruits that had been collected, stored and produced as compotes for the festive occasion. The coffee was a great success and, following dinner, Leonard decided it was the moment for the distribution of his cigarettes. He went into the hall to find his overcoat and, to his horror and puzzlement, found the carton had disappeared. Recollecting his trouble-free journey, Leonard considered there was only one explanation: one of the householders must have taken them. He was seized with rage and, brandishing his privately acquired pistol, dashed back into the room and, in a mixture of English and broken German, forced the household to rise and stand against the wall; no mean feat for the one-legged man. The Hausfrau in particular was shaken by this, proclaiming that they were all to be murdered by the Tommy soldier and on Christmas Day. In fact, Leonard had no intention of shooting anybody, but was determined not to take the theft of two hundred cigarettes lightly. He demanded to know the identity of the culprit and there was a rapid exchange in German that he was unable to follow, culminating in the Hausfrau beating Maria around the head with her handbag until the latter slunk out into the hall, opened a drawer and sheepishly returned with the cigarettes.

The bizarre situation continued. Leonard, with a curt nod of acknowledgement, accepted the cigarettes, before presenting them to the head of the household with his compliments. He put away his pistol and it would appear that the festivities recommenced.

As the bitter night drew on, the Hausfrau invited Leonard to remain for the night, pointing out that he had a long, cold walk back to barracks. Leonard replied that, the cottage being crowded, he was unsure where he would sleep. 'Why, with Maria of course,' came the reply.

Leonard was somewhat startled by this. He could not imagine a similar remark being made by any of the matriarchs of Pontefract with regard to their daughters. Still, perhaps "When in Rome?" But finer, more fastidious, more cautious feelings prevailed. Did he really want to sleep with someone who had tried to rob him and whom he had then forced against a wall at gun point? No, he decided, he did not. So, thanking the woman for her hospitality and muttering something about a roll call, he made his excuses and left.

There is no way of knowing how the affair may have continued, because, shortly afterwards, Leonard's company was moved to the British Sector of Berlin.

In Berlin, Leonard struck up with Ursula. According to Leonard's description, Ursula was a younger, less calculating girl than Maria. She did not have a German husband alive or dead. Leonard did not line up her family against the wall with a firearm, not least because he could not visit her home at all, it being in the American Sector of the city. The citizenry could pass relatively freely between the different zones, but the troops themselves had to remain rigidly within their own boundaries.

Given that Ursula lacked a warm stove to enhance her charms, it must be supposed that the latter themselves were considerable. Sophisticated conversation was difficult. Ursula spoke very little

English and Leonard only a sort of rudimentary, social German. Nonetheless, this did not seem to restrict their relationship overmuch.

However the army was no respecter of romance, and after a few months, Leonard's unit was moved to the Austrian border region. Within two weeks, Leonard received a closely written letter of several pages. However, it was written in formal German script and Leonard could scarcely understand a word of it, other than the signature, "Ursula". How to respond? Leonard only knew a few people sufficiently fluent in German to translate the letter and he was not keen for the probable content to be divulged to any of these. He decided to consider his options, but these were further complicated by a sudden order to embark for Egypt.

It is a compliment to the Forces Postal Service that two similar letters were delivered to him in Africa over the next few months. Each placed him in a quandary. What did they say? How should he respond? Months went by and eventually it seemed too late to make a response at all.

Leonard kept the letters. Perhaps from sentimentality; perhaps he hoped to have them translated someday. However, fifteen years later, the letters were found by his wife in a discreet cranny and their history demanded. They were angrily torn up and burnt and their content never revealed.

Boys and Girls Come Out to Play

It was his wall and she was playing on it. To be precise, the wall was part of the house belonging to their parents or more precisely still, belonging to the Halifax Building Society. To the ten-year-old boy, though, it was indubitably his.

He wanted to practise his cricket shots by throwing a tennis ball against it and hastily playing a forward defensive or drive to the rebound. Cuts and hooks were not normally part of the repertoire owing to the ensuing trudge to retrieve the ball. But here was his stupid sister, playing tennis shots against it.

'Move,' said the boy. 'I need to practise my cricket.'

'Why should I move?' answered his sister. 'I was here first.'

What a stupid girl she was. There were cricket trials tomorrow and he needed to practise.

'I don't care,' he replied. 'Just move.'

'No,' she said. 'I'm practising my backhand.'

He waited until she hit the ball against the wall again, nipped in front of her, caught it and hurled it the length of the drive and onto the road.

'Now just leave me alone.'

Giving a squeak of anguish, the girl ran off to retrieve it.

The boy managed several fine forward defensives shots before her return.

'I'm playing on it,' she said and began to jostle for position.

The boy grabbed the ball and threw it away again, only to find his tiresome sister returning once more.

'If you do that again, I'll tell Mum.'

She would as well and the boy was uncomfortably aware that his mother was so misguided that she might not understand his paramount need to practise.

'No,' he said. 'I'm practising; just keep away.'

That was fair warning, wasn't it? If some stupid girl wanted to push in when he was practising his hook shot for a change, well, that was her fault. He threw a ball that bounced up much more than the norm and hooked it imperiously to the gate, catching his intervening sister full across the face with his follow-through. He felt a twinge of guilt. But he'd told her, hadn't he? Anyway, her nose wasn't bleeding and it hadn't hit her on the mouth. No, it was just her cheek. She ran inside squawking and crying.

'Mum, Mum, Stephen's just hit me in the face with a cricket bat and he meant it; he meant to do it.'

Oh dear, thought the boy as his mother emerged.

'What on earth is going on out here?'

'We were squabbling about the wall and I hit her while I was practising my cricket. I didn't know she was there.'

'He did know; he did it completely on purpose!' wailed the sister.

'You must really learn to play nicely together,' said the mother, 'But Mary, he wouldn't have hit you purposely. No one would do a thing like that. Now, Stephen, say you're sorry.'

It looked as though the wall might be his.

'Sorry,' said the boy dutifully.

It is fair to say the apology was as gracefully accepted as it was genuinely given.

'He's not; he's not!' wailed the sister, storming off as their mother went back inside.

Peace at last, thought the boy, driving the next ball straight past the bowler in a most satisfactory manner.

* * *

A good dig can be very therapeutic and this sand tray was a good one, being well set up with shovels, buckets and rather amusing arrangements of cogs and wheels that spun attractively as sand cascaded through them. The king of these gadgets was being used by some Neanderthal boy.

"Neanderthal" was not a word that featured in the vocabulary of even a linguistically advanced four-year-old girl. This was a pity, because it would have encapsulated Aimee's views on her rival perfectly.

Just look at him, she thought. *He doesn't even know how to use it properly. It's so interesting to watch the sand cascade down and spin, but all he can do is hit it with his spade.*

She tried to take it off him.

'No!' he shouted and gripped it to him.

'Play nicely, Nathan,' called the playgroup leader, glancing across.

For Aimee, though, this was only a preliminary. A minute or two later, she picked up some sand and surreptitiously threw some in his face.

'No!' shouted the boy.

'Nathan, play quietly!' called the playgroup leader, glancing across and seeing Aimee by now industriously building sand castles.

Shortly after this, while Nathan was distracted by a passing fire engine, Aimee quickly snatched the fascinating toy.

Giving a primitive roar of 'No, mine, mine', Nathan launched himself across the sand tray in a desperate attempt to regain possession. Two staff members materialised, pulled Nathan away and restored the sand tray to order.

'Now what's this all about?'

'Mine,' said Nathan, sticking tenaciously to his theme.

'He just tried to grab it,' said Aimee. 'He's still learning to share, isn't he?'

'Nathan,' said the playgroup leader, 'You'd better come with me and sit on this chair until you feel a little bit calmer.'

The cogs and wheels really did look lovely in the sunlight, Aimee thought as she trickled sand through them.

The Great Game

Albert McIntyre was widely thought to be reaching the end of the road. Which road? All of them really. He and his wife had sometimes discussed "if I get run over by a bus" scenarios, but this had not really helped when "the bus" had arrived in the guise of an undetected aneurism and abruptly taken away his wife six months previously.

At work, his end-of-year appraisal had been "satisfactory", which, in these hyperbolic times, was not really good enough. He seemed so much slower than even a year ago and innovation was a stranger to him. The feeling that "at his age, it's time for him to go" was not so much whispered as openly acknowledged. When his children rang, customary discussions about the Lions Tour or the test match score fell flat. It was not that Albert could not remember; he had not been interested enough to find out. Weekends tended to be spent at home, watching whatever presented itself on television.

There were those who tried to be kind to Albert. These included Alison, a much younger work colleague who had joined the firm six years previously. Alison was generally thought to be vivacious, intelligent and attractive. Albert had not been at all immune from the general view and, human nature being what it is, had found himself being rather more sociable than was his wont, the more so when, surprisingly, she appeared to enjoy talking to him.

It appeared that Alison was a nice person who had some genuine regard for Albert, because, even though his creativity, wit and energy had plummeted, she continued to initiate conversation and once noticed and discretely prevented a catastrophic error he was about to make, quietly pointing it out only to him.

It was on the two hundredth night after the aneurism that the dream happened. The Voice spoke to Albert.

'I will offer you two years of prime youthful life. Do you accept my offer?'

The subconscious Albert appeared to have more of its wits about it than the conscious one.

'I've heard about this sort of thing before and no good comes of it.'

'What sort of thing?'

'Well, what about that time you went down to Georgia and I can't even play the violin. Either two years would be it or you'd want my soul or something.'

'A soul? What is a soul? We merely invite people to join our team and many have been allocated to it anyway. But in your case, there are no strings, as you might call them, attached. You get two years of youthful, prime life and then revert to the state you would be in anyway. There is no requirement to act in any particular way and no immortal repercussions.'

'But you must be gaining something.'

'You are a very hard person to please. Most people would jump at my offer, but, though it will temporarily drain my powers, I'll throw in some additional talent with the deal.'

'Talent?'

'No "superpowers", you understand; slightly improved co-ordination, faster recovery and reaction times, a good memory, that sort of thing. Now do you accept or not?'

'And nothing bad will happen to me?'

'Who knows your future? But there are no personally negative consequences attached to the deal; so: Yes or No?'

'Well, yes, all right then, given that nothing bad will happen to me.'

'Your choices are your own as always, but there are no negative consequences linked to the deal; Yes or No?'

'Yes, yes, all right.'

When he woke in the morning, Albert had only a vague recollection of the dream. He remembered it was the day of the Park Run and, for the first time in seven months, felt energetic enough to give it a go. To his astonishment, he was only five seconds outside his best ever time. After a few more attempts, Albert's times were fifteen per cent faster than anything he had achieved in the previous five years. He joined a gym. Shortly after, his muscles seemed definitely more defined and what about his skin? Surely it was less wrinkled and more glowing? And where were those streaks of grey? He reappeared at the tennis club and surprised those present with the positivity of his play. His volleys were spot on and his top spin ground strokes seemed to find the sweet spot with unerring accuracy. The dream was becoming reality.

Within three months, he seemed a changed man. Exercise continued to be a pleasure. He ate sensibly and cut down on his drinking. When his youngest son paid a dutiful visit, he was astonished to find himself challenged to a game of tennis. He tactfully accepted, thinking it would be good for the old fellow to get a bit of exercise again. He had noticed a positive change in body shape, so was not altogether surprised to find his father moving well in the warm-up. What did surprise him was the crispness of the volleying, this having being a traditional area of weakness in the paternal game. His father also seemed to have doubled his normally rather pedestrian service speed, without any loss of its famed reliability. Soon, the young man had lost the first set 2–6, a result unknown since the age of twelve. Surely, though, he had been caught off guard? He'd shrug off his relaxed attitude and matters would definitely be different He gained one more game, losing 3–6, and packed up his kit, a baffled and perplexed young man.

There was one aspect of life Albert was finding difficult to deal with and this was his startlingly increased libido. He hadn't really thought about that sort of thing much during the last six months. Now it seemed to intrude on his mind about every six minutes. He tried to cast his mind back to when he was younger. Had things been this intense? It had been a long time since he was unattached, but he thought not. Could this be some kind of "bonus enhancement" in the same way as his improved hand–eye co-ordination?

It became still more difficult to manage, because he had suddenly become noticeable again. When he had been young and "interested", good-looking young women had tended to look at him in a kind of "Of course you think I'm attractive, but I don't bother with the likes of you" kind of way. However, for around the last twenty years, he had not been noticed at all. It was as though he was invisible. Presumably it was thought impossible for anyone as old and decrepit as he to contemplate such matters. Not now though; women seemed to be continually catching his eye and what had that assistant in the shop meant when she said: "If you want to come in later, it would be a real pleasure?"

He'd never been promiscuous. He now wondered whether this was through morality, restricted opportunity or fear. What if he looked for a "permanent relationship" then? Twenty-one months wasn't very permanent, though, was it? No easy decisions, it seemed.

Albert was, in fact, very mixed up overall. For example, it seemed he could potentially be very good at sport. Should he try to win some titles? He'd have to get a move on if he only had twenty-one months.

He began to find his relationship with Alison more problematic. Any spark of attraction he had felt previously would have had to kindle a libido akin to sludgy paraffin, a task more suited to a blowtorch than a spark. Now the paraffin seemed to have been replaced by rocket fuel. The situation was all the more unstable since he sensed some reluctant reciprocation of feelings. Albert did not really believe in adultery, though, even for himself, and managed to curb his behaviour.

Matters were resolved at the firm's summer barbeque. Albert was deep in conversation at the entrance with a new client and the managing director's family when, as if in slow motion, he saw Emily, the three-year-old daughter of the MD, lose her grip on her balloon and step off the pavement after it.

It was said at the inquest that "only an Olympic athlete could have completed the rescue and hoped to survive". Albert did reach her in time to give her a shove though and, apart from a broken arm where the wheel passed over it, her injuries were mostly superficial. However this was not a word that could be used to describe the effects of the full impact of the bonnet and of the wheels passing over Albert's torso.

'So,' said the Young Spirit, 'It's not at all clear to me. Had The Opposition got this planned all along? Was the deal a blatant swindle?'

'No, it's much more complex,' said the Older Spirit. 'The future is like a game of chess, but much more complex. There are billions of possible outcomes and neither We nor The Opposition can be certain what will happen. We strive for peace, harmony, predictability and so on, while They favour generating raw emotions generally through discord, dispute and devastation. They have to be careful with that last one, though. Too much of it means there are precious few left to dispute.'

'It seems a small action to have bothered taking in the wider scheme of things,' observed the Young Spirit

'These days, it is very difficult for Us or Them to do anything at all,' replied The Elder. 'Mostly, we work through the planting of ideas. Anyway, a major component of The Game is that participants must make their own decisions. Just occasionally, though, power levels are sufficient to induce a small direct change and that is what must have happened in this case.'

'But why would The Opposition have used precious power to do this?'

'An interesting question and we've been running it through our Machine. The Machine can estimate probabilities of certain broad outcomes, some way ahead. We're always trying to improve the efficiency and accuracy of our Machine and I imagine The Opposition are doing the same.'

'And?'

'As far as we can tell, it's all been to do with Alison's putative child.'

'But Alison and her husband haven't got a child.'

'No, and they may never have one, but in many potential futures they do and, in a substantial proportion of those, the child seems to gain substantial political power and influence and to use these as we would wish. The Opposition no doubt hoped to prevent this.'

'Couldn't they just have arranged some accident to befall the child?'

'Their power for direct influence is very small. In any event, a key part of The Game is that outcomes arise from the choices of the participants.'

'So what choices were The Opposition angling for?'

'We believe they wanted to block the conception of the child. Clearly if something had begun between Albert and Alison there would have been marital repercussions.'

'But that's ridiculous. Why choose Albert? Surely there were lots of younger men who might have been influenced to do the tempting?'

'Perhaps her susceptibility quotient is particularly low. Anyway, no doubt they ran it through their version of the Machine and this plan offered the best chance of a successful outcome.'

'But would it have worked?'

'We'll never know, will we? That's one of the fascinations of The Game. Another is that it never stands still, so we'd better get back to work!'

Realisation

Jones was feeling pleasantly relaxed. The boy he had come to review appeared to have turned over a new leaf. Teaching assistants remained unbitten; nothing was swept off tables; the boy had even proved able to read a few words and had held a civilised, if basic conversation. Jones anticipated a pleasant discussion with parents and staff in half an hour's time: "much improved –well done to all concerned" and so on.

In the meantime, he may as well continue observing this literacy lesson. The teacher was a self-confident young woman who held the class well within control. She wore a rather fine silk scarf and various jewels and bangles that seemed to chime precisely with her outfit. Though she might arouse some envy in the staffroom, among those to whom a slender figure and "effortless" co-ordination came less easily, Jones imagined quite a number of girls in the class would like to be similar to Ms Roberts when they grew up.

Ms Roberts was soon directing the class's attention towards the written efforts of Kalahari Group. Jones had not encountered group names based on deserts before and enjoyed the novelty.

'Now, Millie,' said Ms Roberts. 'Let's see what you have written.'

'*Evelyn came to play and she had tea with me and my mummy.*'

'What good writing, Millie,' said Ms Roberts. 'And isn't it lovely, Class 2, when our friends come to play and to talk to us and our mummies?'

So saying, Ms Roberts picked up a book approximately ten times scruffier than Millie's. Its owner, Billy, sat there expectantly, awaiting the acknowledgement he felt his huge effort deserved. Ms Roberts frowned at the book and Jones realised she was having trouble deciphering the offering.

'Can you remind me what it says, Billy?' she asked.

But Billy just sat there. He had written what he had written. There was no need for embellishment.

'Well, we'll come back to you, Billy,' said Ms Roberts.

'Now, Lily, let's see what you have written.'

'*After skool I went to the shops with my mummy and bort a top.*'

'Nice writing, Lily. And isn't it lovely, Class 2, when we can go to the shops with our mummies and choose lovely new clothes for ourselves?'

It would be going too far to say that Jones had begun to empathise with the less stylish staffroom elements. But he did wonder if Ms Roberts would enthuse quite so enthusiastically over a traditional boy's offering such as:

'*I went home and kicked a ball against a wall.*'

Somehow, he couldn't envisage "isn't it lovely, Class 2, when we go home and hone our football skills by repeatedly booting a ball against the wall and trapping it?".

But suddenly it was Billy's turn again. Ms Roberts was trying hard to extract the content of his masterpiece.

'A dunky zz not hsre.'

'What does it say, Billy?' she asked.

Billy, concentrating furiously, finally decoded his own sage effort.

'A donkey is not a horse,' he declared triumphantly.

'No, it isn't, Billy,' said Ms Roberts, looking at him strangely before moving swiftly on to the next group.

Jones, however, was empathising with his own gender. It was seven weeks before Christmas, so naturally nativity play preparations were well underway. This nascent Darwin had given the scenario full consideration and reached this sound and important conclusion regarding the livestock involved and had felt impelled to vouchsafe this key information to his classmates; not for him the trivialities of a new top. Jones would have liked to discuss the situation further with the young man, perhaps asking how this vital realisation had come to him, but duty called at last and off he went for his meeting.

Rin Tin Tin

When Rees was six, he was told that he must have his tonsils and adenoids removed. It turned out that he had to go into hospital, one Thursday tea-time. Rees's main concern was that he would miss *Rin Tin Tin*. Rees's family did not have a television, but each week at 5:25pm, he was allowed to go into his neighbours' house, take off his shoes and watch this canine hero on their television.

Perhaps, he thought, never having been to one, *There will be televisions at the hospital and I can watch it there.*

But no, there were no televisions at the hospital. Rees was taken to a bed. Each bed had a locker by it. Rees noticed that some children had toys in or on their locker, but he hadn't brought any. Luckily, he had some comics to read. His parents told him he should be brave and do as the doctors and nurses asked and that he would be brought home in an ambulance on Sunday. Would they visit? No, that wasn't allowed. So, after his mother gave him a last cuddle, off they went.

The operation was the next day. First, the children had to take off their pyjamas and put on a kind of gown . Then they had to drink a small amount of something horrible while a nurse stood over them. Then the largish group of boys were all taken to a waiting room and it was explained to them that, when their names were called, they would be taken away and operated on. A good half of the boys started to cry, but Rees remembered he had to be brave and didn't.

The morning wore on, with boys being removed from time to time. Rees tried to work out the system being used. Certainly, it did not seem to be alphabetical. When more than half the boys had been removed, Rees asked the returning nurse a question.

'Excuse me, how do you decide who is going to be next? I was just wondering when it might be me. It's not alphabetical, is it?'

The nurse looked at him gravely before deciding he deserved an answer.

'The operations are all the same. We take the noisiest, most troublesome boys first, so you'll be near the end.'

Even at the age of six, it struck Rees that "being brave" might have its disadvantages.

He was the penultimate boy to be operated on. A woman with a mask asked if he could count to twenty.

'Yes, easily,' said Rees.

'Well, I'm going to put this mask on you and I want you to start counting slowly up to twenty.'

'What shall I do if I get to twenty?' asked Rees.

'Don't worry about that; you won't.'

The mask was clamped on and Rees started to count. He thought he could easily get to twenty without being knocked out.

'One... two... three... four... five... six... seven... eight... nine... ten...' Halfway there and he wasn't even a bit sleepy. 'Eleven... twelve... thirteen... fourteen...'

What if I do it, though, and get all the way to twenty, thought Rees. *They might not actually know what to do... I'd better actually try to fall asleep...*

'Fifteen... sixteen... seventeen... eighteen...'

Rees came round in his bed. He had to swill water around in his mouth and spit it out. There wasn't much blood; it didn't hurt much.

Some of the boys were crying again. The nurses were very hard on this, using scorn, bribery and threats to minimise it.

In the evening, the nurses changed over. Most of the other boys fell asleep. Rees began to feel sad. There was no one to talk to and he hadn't seen his mum or dad for a long time. He began to whimper quietly.

'Rees, in bed eleven,' called out a nurse, 'Stop that silly crying or there'll be no jelly and ice cream for you tomorrow.'

Rees was a bit ashamed of himself anyway and nothing hurt very much, did it? The thought of being deprived of the much promised jelly and ice cream, good food for delicate throats, as well as being delicious, was too much to bear. He shut up.

The next day went by very slowly, but at least he did get his jelly and ice cream and, after one more night, it was time to go home.

As he got out of the ambulance, his mum came running down the drive and gave him an enormous cuddle.

'I've made you your favourite meat and potato pie for lunch,' she said.

Rees couldn't eat a lot of it, though, because of the crust.

Flexibility

Rachel preferred working with children, but these days all those opportunities were taken. Her psychological studies had racked up an enormous debt and she regarded it as essential to enter a psychological profession if she was to attain the status and financial freedom she valued. Entry to doctorate courses in, for example, clinical psychology required experience and plenty of it. She had had little success in her approaches to schools, but her application to Golden Sunset had been accepted without undue difficulty and, after a few prosaic checks, here she was.

Rachel proffered the bar code on the badge she had been sent to a code reader and the doors swished open, giving access to a large hall with corridors off. Nothing much seemed to be going on, but it seemed that a security camera must have detected her presence, because a hushed whirring and scuttling announced the approach of one of the facility's robots.

'Transmitting intruder alert,' it announced, rather disconcertingly. 'Threat level estimate low; physical action not presently considered necessary.'

Well, that was something. A second robot arrived.

'Helping to prevent intruder incursion,' it stated determinedly.

A third robot arrived. It appeared to study her closely.

'This is no intruder; it is Rachel,' it explained.

'There are no Rachels; it is an intruder,' retorted the first.

To Rachel's relief, a harassed-looking woman arrived. Speaking very clearly, she enunciated, 'This is not an intruder. This is Rachel. Accept. Accept. Now return to your duties.'

The machines hummed off obediently.

'Good morning, Rachel,' said the woman. 'I'm Melissa and I'm very glad to see another human face, I must say.'

'Aren't there any more staff?' asked Rachel, askance.

'There's Andrea, who I hand over to in the evenings, and we have some back-up staff for holidays and so on. We used to each have an assistant, but they had to go back to Poland and Romania and they never got replaced, though we were sent an extra robot. We've got quite a few now, Wash One and Feed you've just met, oh and Chat Box; she was the more sensible one. Then there's Cookie and Scour – they're all good workers, oh and Washmore and Counsel.'

'And how many... er...?' began Rachel.

'More Senior Citizens Living Enhanced Lives?'

Rachel nodded.

'Fourteen at the moment... Look, I've got quite a lot on just now... Perhaps you'd like to have a look around? You can talk freely to the robots; they've all accepted you now and you can chat to any of the More Senior Citizens, if they seem interested in you. Don't push yourself forward too much, though; some of them need time to get used to change. I'll find you in a couple of hours and we can have a chat. All right?'

Rachel nodded and set off uncertainly down a corridor. Heated words could be heard emerging from a room and she paused to peep around the door. The robots were inscribed with numbers, rather like football players, though more understated. Someone had later stencilled on names. Rachel was encountering "1764 Counsel".

'It is natural, Audrey, for you to miss Colin, your husband,' said Counsel.

'I've never even had a husband,' said the agitated woman, 'And certainly not one called Colin.'

'Denial is a common, but ineffective strategy in the management of grief,' said Counsel. 'Acceptance is the first step in moving on.'

A surprisingly vitriolic outburst emanated from the woman.

'I can sense,' said Counsel, with what dignity it could muster, 'That you are currently overwrought. I will return when you are more open to discussion.' And with this, it trundled through the door.

Rachel moved on swiftly. She peeped through the door of the next room. Chat was just beginning to talk to an elderly male.

'Brian, knowing of your interest in cricket, I have recorded the highlights of yesterday's play on my chest screen, as I noticed you were asleep when they were broadcast live.'

'Well, thank you,' said the mild-mannered old fellow, 'But actually it's golf I follow... if you happen to have recorded the Masters?' But the test match theme tune was already ringing out.

Rachel's attention was diverted by sounds from down the corridor where Wash and Washmore appeared to be gently chivvying a woman from her room.

'Our odour detectors indicate that a thorough wash is highly desirable,' said Washmore.

'Well, maybe, maybe,' replied the woman. 'I can take a hint as well as the next woman, but why can't I do the washing?'

'You do seem surprisingly able-bodied, compared to our normal clientele,' admitted Wash, 'But no doubt you have a hidden impairment, necessitating our involvement. We have definite instructions to proceed.'

Rachel decided to intervene.

'Good morning, Rachel,' said Wash as she approached.

'Can I help?' she asked.

'They're insisting on washing me again,' came the reply.

'And can you really wash yourself?'

'Of course I bloody can!' snapped the irate woman. 'Been doing it for seventy-six years, haven't I?'

'I think I'd better find Melissa,' said Rachel.

'Oh, it doesn't matter. They make quite a good job of it actually and it's quite fun. I just like to make the point. I don't like to become "learned helpless" without a fight.' And the assorted trio moved off.

Rachel decided it really was time to talk to Melissa.

'Oh, hello, I was just about to come and find you,' said Melissa, after Rachel found her in her office. 'It's a bit hectic, isn't it? I don't know what we'd do without the robots; they're so good at what they do. You really should see Scour cleaning the floors.'

'Yes,' said Rachel, 'But I couldn't help noticing that just sometimes the robots seemed slightly on the wrong tack. One patient insisted she'd never been married, another was shown cricket rather than golf and a third was about to be washed when she could manage herself.'

'Oh no, not again,' replied Melissa. 'You see, they come with their basic functions hardwired in. Cookie, for example, knows thousands of recipes and he's a dab hand with a whisk. But they are part programmable. We're supposed to feed in patient details from a database so they can recognise a patient and remember their preferences and conditions, but there seems to be some kind of glitch in the programme sometimes and somehow the information gets mixed and they end up trying to discuss tennis with someone who hates the game. I had to get onto HQ last week when Cookie made a delicious cake for Ronny, who's a chronic diabetic. They've been promising to correct the glitch for months now, but nothing's happened yet. I can't override patient information myself; it's fed to them from HQ.'

'Can't you contact them again?' asked Rachel.

'Well, it's just been really hard, with me here on my own during the day; there's just so much to do.

Also, I don't really want to upset them. My contract's up for renewal in two months and I don't want to get on the wrong side of anyone.'

Rachel knew all about the importance of not ruffling feathers from the completion of her PhD: "'No' – Imperative or Initial Point of Negotiation? Variation in the Comprehension of the Prohibitive in the 3–5 Year Age Range". The effort to get it past the ethics committee and to mollify and flatter her tutors sufficiently had been immense. This was different, though. That had been a calculation, a hoop to get through to gain a qualification. This involved real people. Rachel was surprised and rather pleased to find herself getting angry.

'Well, what about their relations? Surely there have been complaints?'

'You'd be surprised how rare visits are. They know their relatives are in safe hands.'

'Well, can I ring HQ up? I'll try to seem a bit naive and keep you out of it.'

'Oh, I suppose so. Here's the number and good luck.'

Rachel went into the adjoining room and phoned.

'Thank you for calling; dealing with your call appropriately is essential to our well-being,' said a disembodied voice. 'If you wish to purchase a team of robots for your care facility, press 1; if you want to book a regular service for your robot team , press 2; if you wish to book a demonstration of our robot team at our high-tech production facility, press 3; for all other enquiries, please press 4.'

Rachel dutifully pressed 4 and received the message "we apologise for the wait. This is due to an unusually high number of calls today; you are currently number 17 in the queue; please hold on or call back later...".

Bugger, thought Rachel succinctly. What could she do?

There on the desk top was a glossy brochure advertising Transformational Robotic Care Services, with the Chief Executive, Bill Priestley beaming in a solicitous and focused manner from the front cover.

Rachel went off in search of Chat and found her discussing the niceties of bridge with a bewildered elderly flower arranger.

'Chat,' said Rachel, 'Must you do as I ask?'

Chat contemplated gravely.

'You may make suggestions, Rachel, and I will carry these out if they do not contradict my basic programming or diverge from instructions from the Hierarchical Organisational Group.'

'Is Melissa a member of the Hierarchical Organisational Group?'

'Yes indeed. She is HOG 7. Her instructions can be overridden by HOGs 1–6, but take precedence over those of HOG 8.'

'Could you tell me the names of the HOGs please?'

Rachel was pleased to find that HOG 3 was a female, Olivia Golding.

'Do you know what the HOGs look like?' she asked.

'I have been privileged to meet HOGs 5, 7 and 8. HOG 6 is new in post. Photographs of the HOGs are intended to be on the database, but this remains a work in progress.'

'You robots can all communicate with each other, can't you?' enquired Rachel.

'Our wireless communication is highly developed and helps us to work extremely efficiently and effectively as a well co-ordinated team,' spouted Chat, regurgitating a phrase Rachel had seen in the brochure. 'We communicate new information frequently.'

'Do you know what an alias is?' asked Rachel.

'No.'

'It is another name a person can have. A person can have two names.'

'I did not know this. Do many people have aliases?'

'Oh lots,' said Rachel. 'Try looking up the names of film stars.' She left Chat to continue stressing the importance of taking out trumps.

A few days later, Rachel asked Mellissa if she could come back that evening to meet Andrea and to see how the Senior Citizens Living Enhanced Lives spent their evenings.

'Yeah, that's fine,' said Mellissa. 'I'll email to let her know – I'd better print it off as well to make sure she sees it first thing – she can be a bit slow getting up to speed with her emails sometimes.'

'Thanks', said Rachel and sat down at an adjoining desk ostensibly to write up some notes. It was usual for Mellissa to be called away from her desk on all sorts of issues and today was no exception.

Immediately she was gone, before the screensaver was up and security enabled, Rachel was at the machine, substituting the name Olivia Golding for her own and reprinting the email and substituting it for the old one. Then, after a few more judicious changes, preparations were complete.

That evening, Rachel quietly let herself in, established that Andrea was in her office and quietly sought out Chat, who was discussing the possible ramifications of an East Enders plot line with a resident who had never watched it.

'Chat, would you mind taking me to Andrea, as I'm not certain what she looks like?'

'Of course, Rachel, said Chat. 'Mr Norman seems strangely uninterested in East Enders at present.' So off they went.

Rachel was pleased to find that Andrea was just the sort of well-meaning, but uninquisitive individual she hoped she would be.

'Oh hello,' she said, rather flustered and glancing at the paper. 'You must be Olivia Golding.' Evidently, she was not familiar with the name of HOG 3.

Chat looked as surprised as a robot could do.

'Yes,' said Rachel quickly. 'I'm just here for an hour if that's okay, just to see what happens in the evenings.'

'Yes, just carry on,' said Andrea with the air of someone having a lot else to think about.

'Thanks,' said Rachel and moved to the door, accompanied by Chat.

'I do not understand,' he queried as she hustled him down the corridor. 'Are you Rachel or Olivia Golding?'

'I am Olivia Golding', said Rachel. 'Rachel is my alias.'

Chat scanned his memory banks.

'Alias? Ah yes, now I understand.'

'I am HOG 3, Olivia Golding,' said Rachel. 'Please inform the others. Tell them they should still refer to me by my alias, Rachel, but must follow my instructions in accordance with usual hierarchical procedures.'

'It is done already,' said Chat.

'Now,' Rachel explained, 'First, we will visit Brian. Brian has developed a new interest in golf and you should focus on that rather than cricket. Is that possible?'

'Were you aware,' asked Chat, 'That The Masters in Augusta is underway and that three British players are placed in the top twenty?'

'Excellent,' said Rachel.

Next, Rachel summoned Counsel.

'Counsel,' she said, 'It has been decided that Audrey has received enough counselling regarding Colin and you should concentrate your efforts elsewhere.'

'Of course, Olivia,' replied Counsel.

Rachel spent the next two hours correcting other "misunderstandings". She found it all very enjoyable and worthwhile.

It seems I might be more cut out for this area of work than I imagined, she thought.

In the Mood

Anthea's partner had left her. He'd told her one day after fixing the guttering on the garage. He'd thought it "only fair" apparently to tidy up a bit and get things running smoothly before he left.

Anthea had managed to react with dignity. She hadn't hauled all of his clothes out of the wardrobe and set fire to them in the garden. She hadn't attacked him with the nearest household implement. She hadn't even insisted that he leave the house that very day.

She had questioned him, of course. It was all so sickeningly predictable. He'd met Stephanie in a pub in Ludlow, on one of those days when he'd wanted to unwind after a hard day unsuccessfully trying to sell windows. They'd just "hit it off really well" seemingly and, despite "knowing he shouldn't", they had continued to meet, presumably, thought Anthea, during some of those times she'd worked overtime on Saturdays to help keep the mortgage under control.

He had been surprisingly diligent in covering his tracks. There had been some falling off of their sex life, but Anthea had put this down to general sluggishness, not the necessity of harvesting his limited resources for set tos with another woman.

Entirely predictably, she was a few years younger than Anthea and a "former model'", whatever that might mean. Conveniently, she lived alone in a small house about ten miles away. Ha! Anthea liked the sound of "small". She wouldn't want to be cooped up with him in some place with only two bedrooms, a kitchen/diner and a small lounge. She didn't see it lasting and, if not, it would serve him right. What would he do then? Anthea squashed down a ridiculous surge of temporary potential sympathy. No, he wouldn't be coming back; she'd have "moved on". He could fall asleep mid-programme and snore on someone else's sofa.

"Moving on" turns out to be quite difficult in your fifties. Anthea did not have children and thoughts of a possible lonely future kept insinuating themselves into Anthea's mind, though she battled to keep them at bay. Well-meaning friends invited her to parties where they had dredged up the only similarly aged single man they knew. Anthea did not feel she had "signed off" with regard to potential relationships. However, she did not relish her only slightly overweight figure being appraised by some random man, with his own copious gut overhanging the table.

Was the game worth the candle? she wondered. Or, to be more precise, was potential companionship and sex, worth, not so much the ironing of shirts and so on, but the necessity to feign agreement with, or at least be tactful about, pompously expressed views on everything from world affairs to the mundanities of household management? At present, she thought not. Perhaps, though, her views would change? Perhaps there might be some presentable, unattached man who could be both more amusing and less certain than most of his gender and age.

Christmas approached. Anthea was not spending this at home, staring sadly at a small Christmas tree. She was visiting her sister and her adult niece and Anthea expected to have a good time.

As a preliminary, in order to burgeon the Christmas spirit, Anthea visited a nearby National Trust house, spectacularly decorated in the manner of a 1930s Christmas.

As Anthea was staring at the seventh lavishly decorated Christmas tree, a slight commotion at the end of the room heralded the entrance of a teenage girl, ten middle-aged women and a man with the unfortunate look of a closet Morris dancer. There was to be a Charleston demonstration.

The assorted throng made quite a good fist of it. They were mostly in time (as far as Anthea could tell) and had every appearance of enjoying themselves. The ratio of eleven women to one man did not seem too incongruous as dancing individually as part of the ensemble was fine with this kind of music.

It transpired that the display also functioned as a kind of advert for the troupe leader. She spread out pamphlets for "beginners" and "improvers" and Anthea took one. "*Eight one-hour sessions, for £50, 6:30–7:30, beginning on Tues., 5 January.*" Well, it seemed worth a go.

Anthea had been a good mover in the days when she'd gone clubbing and she was pleased to find that at least some of the old magic still remained; more so than with most of the other women anyway. Some could remember the steps, but galumphed rather than shimmied; others could move, but all too often in the wrong direction. None of this was stressed, though. The point seemed to be to enjoy themselves in an uninhibited fashion, away from their partners and husbands, who were generally skulking at home.

Anthea progressed into "intermediates", in which she recognised several members of the original troupe.

She doubtfully had a post-session coffee with the suspected ex-Morris dancer. He seemed to enjoy telling her he was a confirmed Everton supporter and hadn't missed a home game for thirteen years.

No wonder you're unattached, thought Anthea.

She did not say this, partly out of kindness, but mostly because there was very little conversational space in which she could say anything at all. Apparently he had recently hit a four iron two hundred and sixty-eight metres. Despite this evidence of sporting prowess, Anthea decided there would be no further tête-à-têtes.

During intermediate Session 5, an unfortunate incident occurred. Despite her "intermediate" status, a large woman shimmied and bounded left rather than right. Oil tankers take time to lose momentum, even when brakes are applied, and unfortunately the teenage member of the troupe was effectively shoulder charged mid-bound. She disappeared off the stage in spectacular fashion and was discovered on the floor, in tears, clutching her shoulder. Anthea suspected it was dislocated. A lot of concern was expressed, but little offered in the form of practical help.

Anthea managed to establish from the weeping girl that she had intended to go round to her friend's house after the class, from where her father, who was working late, would be picking her up. Anthea thought she had little choice but to take her to hospital and her heart sank as she saw the packed waiting room. They were triaged and it was plain that the shoulder was no one's idea of a life-threatening emergency. The wait would be considerable.

It was fortunate that it was the girl's left shoulder that had met the auditorium floor, as this seemed to leave her free to text, which she did, copiously, with plenty of buzzing indicating frequent replies. The girl, calmer now, at least when still, looked up.

'Thank you very much for helping me, but you don't have to wait; my dad's coming and I won't be seen for ages.'

'What about your mum; couldn't she come?'

'Oh, she lives in Italy these days; great for holidays, but not so good at times like this. You really can go; it doesn't hurt unless I twist it.'

Anthea decided leaving may indeed be a possibility.

'Well, if you're really okay, I suppose I could go.'

'I definitely am and thank you very much for bringing me in.'

The following week, the girl wasn't there.

Broken collar bone or dislocated shoulder I expect, thought Anthea, taking care to place herself well clear of the large woman with directional issues.

'Excuse me,' said a voice. 'I just came to explain to Mrs McAvoy that my daughter won't be attending the last three sessions, but I just wanted to thank you for taking her to hospital last week.'

Anthea looked around. A passably good-looking man was staring at her earnestly.

'That's quite all right. How is Emily?'

'She's got a cracked collar bone. It could have been a lot worse. She was still keen to come, but I didn't want to risk it being made worse. She's very enthusiastic, though, and wants to keep up.'

'Well,' said Anthea, 'I suppose I could always come around and demonstrate the new moves.'

Chinese Whispers

Evans was in difficulty with the younger members of his family. Though he had never "blacked up", he had admitted to once camping it up as a supposedly gay photographer at a murder dinner party. He had also pretended to be deaf (though reluctantly and at his university's request) in order to examine the reaction of shopkeepers to basic sign language. He was pleased that it had been a friend, rather than he, who had pretended to be physically disabled in order to get into a night club. (Chaos had ensued when the wheelchair had rolled down a flight of stairs and his friend had "bailed out" in a blatantly able-bodied way.) The most strident criticism had arisen, however, when, in a spirit of honesty, he had admitted to being part of a crowd, fifty years ago, that had monkey chanted at a fearsome and talented black winger, in a forlorn effort to put him off his game. If he had not participated himself, he had not objected or walked out. The winger had scored two tries and his contribution had essentially been the difference between victory and defeat for his team. In later days, with the approval of the whole Rugby League community, a statue had been erected at his own ground to commemorate his immense contribution to the club and the game in general. Evans was rather ashamed of his tacit adolescent participation, but was nonetheless startled to hear, that according to younger family members, he would be deemed "unfit for public office". He was also puzzled, because, in relation to his peers, Evans thought that on the whole he had behaved rather well during his youth. It wasn't he, for example, who had been arrested by police for attempting to steal roadside traffic lights while drunk, "because I thought they'd look good in my room, Officer". Hadn't they almost all behaved inappropriately in some way and not just by walking through wheat fields? However, as he did not have the energy, commitment or self-confidence to stand for public office, the verdict seemed academic.

For his own peace of mind, though, Evans wanted to find a counterweight to his more inappropriate behaviours. His mind wandered back to his school days.

When he was ten years old, Evans had been summoned to his headmaster's study.

'Next week, a new boy will be starting in your class,' the headmaster had said. 'His name is Fa Sin Liu and he speaks very little English. I would like you to take him under your wing and to help him settle in. Show him how things work and so on. I'll introduce you to him on Monday.'

Liu turned out to be quite a big lad. Some said later that he was considerably older than normal junior age, but this did not occur to Evans at the time.

Evans did not mind his role for the first week or so. He showed Liu the dining room, indicated when it was break time and so on. By week two, it was more irksome. He couldn't play with his friends as much. Liu would often ask Evans about English vocabulary, often via pictures or gesture, and this could get uncomfortable, particularly when he seemed to be straying into the area of body parts and bodily functions.

Liu's English gradually improved, however, until he could use short phrases and he must have been pleased with Evan's help, because one day he asked, :

'You come eat restaurant? Parents say you good – come eat restaurant.'

Evans was confounded by this. The most exotic item in his diet was Lancashire Hotpot. Even Sussex Pond Pudding was unknown to him. He knew nothing about Chinese cuisine and wasn't anxious to know more. What if they gave him something he hated and couldn't eat? He consulted his parents.

'I think you ought to go,' said his mother. 'It's kind of them to invite you and it would be rude to refuse. There's bound to be something on the menu you could eat.'

So one day, straight after school, Evans went. The restaurant was empty apart from him and he had the full attention of three Chinese waiters who bowed him in, but who spoke very little English. Liu's father came out briefly and welcomed him, but there was no sign of Liu himself. Evans had a plate of chips and three bowls of apple pie and custard. If asked to critique the latter, Evans's view would have been: 'Not as good as my mum's, but definitely all right.'

Perhaps the waiters thought his choice unusual, but if so they did not show it and bowed him out with considerable ceremony at the end.

After several more months, Evans was surprised to be approached at school by a rather nondescript, but unpleasant youth called Baxter.

'A word,' he said. 'Keep away from Liu at lunchtime. We're going to get him. He shouldn't be here. He needs to get back where he came from. We've nothing against you, though, so just keep out of the way.'

Evans decided he was not going to "just keep out of the way". After the passage of all the years, the older Evans found it hard to recollect the reasoning behind his decision. He wasn't especially friendly with Liu. Was it because he'd told the headmaster he'd look after Liu? Was it because it just didn't seem fair? Or was it just that Baxter was so obnoxious? Perhaps Liu's reaction when Evans managed to convey the plot to him also helped.

'Me fight, yes; you fight, no.'

Whatever the reason, Evans didn't think he could leave Liu facing "High Noon" alone.

In the event, things went better than expected. Liu shrewdly kept to a small area of the playground so that he could make his stand on the raised entry to a deserted classroom, where two sets of steps led to a small platform. Also two of Evans's friends stood with them. When Horatius held the bridge, his friends were portrayed as solemn, serious and brave:

Then out spake Spurious Lartius,
A Ramnian proud was he,
'Lo, I will stand at thy right hand
And keep the bridge with thee.'
And out spake strong Herminius
Of Titian blood was he,
'I will abide on thy left side
And keep the bridge with thee.'

Evans's friends thought differently. Namely that it was "a bloody stupid thing to do" and that they resented being forced into it, "but we can't very well leave you today and claim to be your mates tomorrow, can we?"

Four against thirty then, but in a bottleneck and Evans was pleased to see that none of the school's top half dozen fighters were among the mob either. Perhaps they disliked the cause or were also loath to seem to be at Baxter's beck and call.

Although fighting was common at Evans's school and staff intervention slow, if it happened at all, this fracas was on a rather different scale to the one-on-one encounters that seemed to be tacitly regarded as "all part of life's rich tapestry". Also, fortunately, there were a couple of other, less martial boys, who were unhappy about the situation and who informed staff of a "big fight" almost immediately. It was only three or four minutes, therefore, before staff arrived to put a stop to the situation and no serious damage was done.

Various boys were questioned by the headmaster afterwards, but no detail was divulged; "it just happened all of a sudden" and so on.

Shortly after this, Liu suddenly left the school. Evans, along with everyone else, was told he wouldn't be returning. But he knew no more. Liu had given no warning of his imminent departure and Evans never learnt where he had gone or ever came across him again.

Evans's mind crossed the fifty year divide to the present. He was not at all sure he would be prepared to make a similar stand now. Perhaps he was now more enlightened in theory, but not in practice?

Difficult to Accept

For a man in a long post office Christmas queue, Rees was in a surprisingly benign mood. He was in no particular hurry and could occupy himself by messaging a friend or two and changing his fantasy football team.

Twenty minutes later, though, he was beginning to wonder whether he had shown all the patience that could reasonably be expected, even of a man of mature years. His intention was to post a peculiarly shaped Christmas parcel on behalf of his wife to a friend in Oxford. It seemed to resemble a kind of asymmetric pyramid with the top sliced off and a peculiar bulge attached to one side. Apart from the hatchet-faced woman on the currency counter, there were two post office employees servicing the long, winding queue. Rees could only suppose that the head of the post office had been extremely moved by some Age Concern advert emphasising the potential loneliness of the elderly during the festive period. Certainly her staff appeared to have received copious training in making the older customer feel valued and in ensuring that, if this was to be their only meaningful social interaction of the day, then it would be full and worthwhile.

'Now, just let me explain it again, dear... Wait a minute, though; I think I'll just check... I think if you're lucky it'll count as a large letter rather than a small parcel and that would save you a bit, my dear.... It needs to be able to fit through here, you see...'

The woman produced a large piece of plastic with a slot in the middle.

'Yes, we're in luck; it will go through... and it weighs... well, that's fortunate; just under 500g. So these are your options, my love: second class £1.58 and first class £1.74... but of course if there's anything valuable in it and you want to have it tracked and signed for, well, second class would be £2.68 and first class, £2.84. And you have left yourself plenty of time, haven't you, my dear? Because if it needed to get there in the next day or two, we could look at some more options, but they'd be over £7, which is a lot to post a parcel, isn't it, my dear?'

'Well,' said the elderly lady, 'It just needs to get there by Christmas; it's for my daughter and she lives down in Kent, so I won't be seeing her , but my son lives in Birmingham and he'll be coming over... £7 did you say? That does seem a lot of money...'

'No, no, my dear, you don't need to spend £7; first or second class will be fine...'

Fortunately, Rees was spared the next part of the conversation by the arrival of his wife, who had been carrying out some transactions at the bank.

'Goodness, are you still in the queue?' she asked.

Rees glanced around just slightly. He wanted to convey a soupcon of the Basil Fawlty style. 'Oh yes dear, do you know, I think I still am.' But not to the extent that he could not plausibly deny it. He also felt nettled at the faintly implied criticism. After all, he was not the manager of the post office. It was not he who had decided that the presence of a mere two-counter staff and a hatchet-faced woman was sufficient in the busy Christmas period. It was not he who had decided that all elderly customers should have all options explained to them repeatedly and at great length.

'Well, it'll be nice for you to see your son anyway, my dear,' floated through his reverie.

Perhaps, pondered Rees, his wife thought he should have shouldered aside a few of the more frail old ladies and joined the queue halfway up? And it was, of course, his wife's parcel… Still, it was the season of goodwill and he forbore to comment.

'Well, it looks as though you'll be some time yet,' she said appraisingly.

Rees let a blink accompany the slightly querulous look that he adopted for the invisible audience he sometimes envisaged looking on. This was meant to imply that, until now, the truth of this assertion had not struck him.

'I think I'll just go and have another look at that coat in Marks and Spencers.' And with that, she swept off.

However, progress was being made. A third serving station light suddenly came on. At service station one, the end seemed to be in sight, if not yet imminent.

'A pleasure to see you, my dear... Now you go home and have a nice cup of tea and be careful on those pavements; there's still quite a lot of ice about...'

Within ten minutes, Rees found himself at the head of the queue. The HFW, not having any purchasers for euros or dollars, had seemingly been instructed to offer a more general service and it was her light that flashed up.

'I'd like to post this parcel, second class to Oxford,' said Rees. For his time in the queue had not been entirely wasted and he knew his options.

'And what's in it?' asked the HFW.

Rees would have liked to retort "I'm asking you to deliver it, not appraise its contents", but decided this would not be a good idea. He realised with a shock that he did not actually know the answer to this knotty question. He had some recollection of his wife saying: "This would be lovely for Julia, wouldn't it?" But he had not been giving the matter his full attention and today had just accepted his errand without further questions.

Rees was not so slow and not so scrupulous that he did not realise that what was required here was a blatant and plausible lie. That word "plausible" was a touch tricky, though, wasn't it? The first two possibilities that passed through his mind were "a book" or "some chocolates". These items, however, were not generally shaped like lumpy decapitated pyramids. What was, though? The seconds ticked by. Too late now...

'I don't know,' said Rees, truthfully, but weakly.

'Aha,' said the HFW, with a voice, which seemed to Rees, to be awash with triumph. 'Well, if I'm not informed what's in it, I can't accept it.'

To be truthful, the "aha" may not have actually been present in the utterance, but, if not, the tone certainly implied it.

'I'm posting it for my wife,' explained Rees, 'To her friend in Oxford and I've forgotten what's in it, but it's entirely harmless.'

The HFW had heard about husbands and this pathetic ineptitude accorded well with the rumours.

'Has it got batteries?' she snapped.

'No,' said Rees, accepting his cue.

'What about alcohol or lighter fuel.'

'No,' said Rees, confident he had surmounted another hurdle.

'Is it a firearm of some kind?'

With a colossal effort, Rees controlled himself, successfully suppressing all tendencies to irony and sarcasm.

'No,' he replied. 'I remember it's nothing at all controversial.'

The woman wavered slightly. Of course, there was the unfortunate woman married to this inept fellow to consider and indeed her friend, who could potentially be left without a present.

As the scales wavered, Rees wondered whether to point out that, if he really were an unusual English, white, male, elderly terrorist, then wouldn't he have contrived to make his "device" a more normal shape and wouldn't he have arrived with a ready, plausible story?

No, he concluded; better to await the verdict of the HFW. He could always rejoin the queue, he supposed, and shuffle about to avoid this particular station and come up with a more believable story about the content. However, he hoped this could be avoided. In addition to using up another half an hour of his time, he did not relish having to explain to his wife why he was now further back in the queue than he had been when she had left. His reverie was interrupted.

'All right,' said the HFW. 'You can put it on the scales.'

And so it was that Julia did successfully receive her box of artistic Christmas baubles, though what the lump was, Rees never knew.*

* *Editor's note:* A sumptuous flower attached to the internal wrapping to make the gift still more attractive...

Artistic Drive

City breaks often entailed a visit to a gallery. In his younger days, Rees must have supposed that a burgeoning knowledge and appreciation of art was possible, if not probable. Now in secondary middle age, he knew better. He generally scurried past sixteenth and fifteenth century religious pictures, with or without perspective, in favour of a good long stare at two or three Impressionist paintings or the study of an occasional portrait, his particular favourite being *The Skating Minister* by Raeburn in the National Gallery of Scotland.

Rees enjoyed contemplating the mind-set of the austere looking clergymen, who, after a Sunday morning inveighing against the various temptations of the flesh, must have then uttered the Presbyterian equivalent of:

'But enough of this; where's my skates? I'm off to hurtle around the lake again; it's just so tremendously exhilarating.'

It was not just the mind-set of the clergyman that Rees attempted to contemplate. Plenty of other subjects invited similar, if not quite so fascinating, analysis; and not only the subjects, but also the artists, for example the Pre-Raphaelites.

Rees had never had a muse, as seemed *de rigueur* for any self-respecting Pre-Raphaelite. As far as Rees could make out, these were attractive young women who were painted by day and by night... well, no doubt you can imagine that part.

What were the predominant characteristics in himself that had inhibited muse acquisition? Rees wondered. Contentment? morality? Well, let's hope so. But could it be chiefly just dullness, combined, perhaps, with a little too much honesty and self-appraisal? For it must have taken some over-whelming audacity and supreme actual or simulated self-confidence to persuasively assert that some heavy bouts of musing were absolutely necessary to produce the works of genius that the world would be so much the poorer without.

It was possible, thought Rees, to the modern mind, that the young women were not as gullible as sometimes portrayed and that they accepted all the muse/genius protestations with a pinch of salt, being all too happy to cavort with a handsome young painter. One day, however, Rees realised that this possibility was all too simplistic.

In a Pre-Raphaelite exhibition, he read the back-ground to *Ophelia*. In order to get the right effect, Millais had persuaded his model, Elizabeth Siddall, to lie in a bath of water for days on end. It appeared that it was his intention to heat the bath with oil lamps, but he "often forgot". Rees could not im-agine ever having been able to persuade any young woman he had ever known to lie in a cold bath even for an hour or so while he tried to paint her. No, credit where it was due, these chaps were obviously awash with much more mesmerising artistic temperament than he himself had ever possessed. He took some comfort though, from learning that Elizabeth's father had grumpily gone round and demanded payment for the medical bills run up by the illnesses, allegedly caused by prolonged immersion in the bath.

Artistic drive and determination had sometimes shown themselves in ways harder to fathom. In Lisbon, Rees had visited Igreja da SaoVicente de Fara, a sparkling white monastery with splendid views and much to admire. On the walls of an upper storey, however, made from blue and white tiles, are the *Fables of Fontaine*, with accompanying commentaries. These are somewhat bleak for modern taste; e.g.:

A wolf got a bone stuck in his throat and asked a stork to remove it with the aid of his long beak. The stork did so and suggested some reward. 'It should be enough,' said the wolf, 'For you to boast that you have successfully placed your beak in my throat and removed it again. You should not expect more.'

Just who had driven this project forward? Was the abbot a renowned admirer of La Fontaine? Had he had to bring it up at committee and ask for suggestions regarding wall art? Was he sufficiently autocratic, by nature or position, to push the project through, perhaps quelling with a single glare the suggestion that thirty-five might be almost three dozen too many?

How was funding obtained? Did lots of tiling firms tender for the job?

Above all, with what real or simulated enthusiasm was the finished product reviewed?

Rees suspected that if it were unveiled today, comments might reflect his own views: 'There's rather a lot of them, aren't there?' Or, 'I wonder if they could have included a few more colours?' Or, 'He was a bit gloomy, really, wasn't he, La Fontaine?'

Perhaps, though, in earlier times, as the throng battled to get in for a first viewing, the following comments might have been heard among the jostling multitude:

'I hope they've got the one about the two dogs from the same litter brought up differently.'

Or, 'My favourite's the one about the two goats dying on a bridge, because neither will give way – a lesson to us all.'

But Rees knew he would never know. Fascinating though, it was to speculate, it was impossible for him to simulate the eighteenth century Portuguese mind-set.

The Balcony

The reader must not feel concerned. It is true that Rees was not whistling a merry tune and feeling that all was right with his world, but only because he was asleep, with his wife, similarly contented, a foot to his left.

The pair had arrived at their Welsh seafront flat late that evening, found it in good order and gone straight to bed. The weather forecast was predicting high temperatures and sunshine for the next few days. It appeared that for once the Arctic fleeces and trawler standard wet wear, with which the wardrobe was packed, would remain unused.

The position to Rees's left has already been sketched out. Immediately to his right was a patio door leading to a narrow balcony that ran, uninterrupted, along the length of the Victorian terrace. In deference to the unusual warmth of the night, the door had been left open and through it floated the sounds of small waves politely tumbling onto the sandy beach.

Suddenly, though, the murmuring of the waves was drowned by a tremendous kerfuffle from the balcony outside. Rees awoke, startled. The word "kerfuffle" is a useful catch-all, but perhaps something more specific is required. The sounds included large-scale scrabbling, gruff vocalisation, elements of tapping and stamping, together with a kind of ominous rustling sound. It seemed amazing to Rees that, despite A Mystery Creature practically being in bed with them, his wife slept on, blissfully unaware of all the commotion.

Rees pondered on what could be – I was going to say "lurking", but lurking it certainly wasn't – putting itself about so grumpily on his balcony. His best guess was something owned by Daenerys Queen of Dragons, considerably past the hatching phase, but stopping short of army incinerating adulthood.

He knew he was procrastinating. Rees's household was a traditional one. He was pleased to have most of his meals made for him and his shirts ironed when necessary. However, when it came to moving dead rabbits, catching moles or clearing gutters, the responsibility had always been his. Perhaps if he was married to a New Woman, Rees thought, she might have said: 'You stay here, darling, snuggled in your bed, while I go into mortal combat with The Creature on the Balcony.' No chance of that, though, especially given that unbelievably, despite the crashing sounds outside, his wife still slumbered on. No, he had made his bed and he would have to lie in it; or the opposite rather. So Rees hauled himself out from under his quilt and, clad only in his boxer-style pyjama bottoms, pushed through the patio door and – well, I was going to say "strode", but, more accurately, tiptoed out onto the balcony.

Now there may be some readers who have entered into close quarters combat with an angry she seagull on a narrow balcony and, if you are one of these, please feel free to skip the next few paragraphs. For those who haven't though, a seagull in the prime of life, with its wings spread, its beak snapping and uttering its fearsome battle cry, is no mean adversary. Those readers less experienced in seagull combat might also be interested to know that, rather like swans, seagulls need a bit of a run-up to take off and it was this factor that caused matters to proceed rather in the manner of a fencing scene from an old Errol Flynn movie. Rees would advance down the balcony, shouting haplessly. The bird would retreat before him, try to take off and smash ineffectually into the end balcony partition. Then, roused by anger and desperation, it would turn and charge, determined to show to whom this balcony really belonged. Rees, remembering the reputation of the seagull species for snatching chips and sausages with their cruel hooked beaks, would worry about which parts of his anatomy, to say nothing of his eyes, were vulnerable and retreat, until, asking himself if he was a man or a fish, he would return to the charge.

Despite being hard-pressed, Rees had some scruples and bridled from giving the thing a hefty kick (and besides, he was only in bare feet – bear in mind if doing something similar, be properly shod). Eventually, though, as the beast came to close quarters, he managed to get his shin beneath it and lift it a foot or two into the air. Feeling it had done enough to preserve its honour, the seagull condescended to fly off, leaving Rees in possession of the field.

Rees had read Ivanhoe and knew that the victor in single combat traditionally received the praise of a fair lady, generally accompanied by a token of her appreciation. He had expected that even his wife would have woken at least in a "1906, Oh has there been an earthquake" kind of way, but no, she slept on, oblivious to his prowess, and so Rees received no appreciative welcome. He crawled back under the quilt and, as the adrenaline lessened, found himself drifting back to sleep.

Rees awoke early in the morning and, aware of some significant, but more distant scuttling, poked his head through the patio doors and peered over the balcony partition to next door. He spotted three well-grown seagull chicks strutting about amidst a filth of droppings, feathers and half-digested fish. Mrs Seagull was perched on the neighbours' balcony railings, looking fondly at her brood, while letting the world know what she thought of her harsh treatment during the night. Presumably, thought Rees, she had flown off during the night for essential supplies, landed on the wrong balcony and then, in her flustered state, had had difficulty getting off again and returning to her chicks.

Rees decided his first job was to reinforce the partition between the two balconies and, after breakfast, he began to do this with various makeshift materials. The chicks were large, ugly creatures, reminiscent of small vultures, though with shorter necks. They were already strutting and fluttering about. It seemed a toss-up whether, wondering if the grass was greener, they would attempt to squeeze through the bars of the partition or flutter over it. In his quest for a guano-free balcony, Rees could at least strive to safeguard against the former.

It turned out that the neighbours were not away, as Rees had supposed. They had ceded the balcony to the seagulls and moved to the back bedroom, leaving their usual bedroom as a kind of no man's land. The neighbour explained that they had contacted both the council and the RSPCB and received advice that "the birds were best left where they were". Good advice, thought Rees, from twenty miles away, if it isn't your balcony being turned into a bird sewer or you being kept awake.

Over the course of the day, it turned out that the beachside inhabitants thought of themselves as some sort of proxy owners/carers for the birds. Rees was asked to speculate about how long it would be before they could fly. Others accosted him in the street and hoped he was giving them plenty of water. Rees expected to be advised at any moment to nip down to the fish shop and get some nice pieces of haddock to chew up for them.

Rees and his wife were expecting visitors and Colin and Marian duly arrived. It would have been nice to go out onto the balcony from time to time, but unwise. In return for this concession, Mrs Seagull allowed Rees to pass a quieter night. Some kind of Korean impasse appeared to have been reached, with the balcony divider serving as the thirty-eighth parallel north.

The next day dawned even hotter and there was precious little shelter on the balconies. Although

Rees wanted to be rid of the birds, he didn't want them to die a horrible death from heatstroke or dehydration either. It seemed highly questionable whether, even from their own perspective, the birds were "better off where they are". Some plastic chairs appeared on the neighbouring balcony beneath which some respite could be found from the sun.

Matters came to a head as the group returned from a game of putting. Two baby seagulls had made "The Great Leap Forward" onto Rees's balcony. The neighbours appeared to have gone. *Might they have furtively slipped them over?* Rees wondered, uncharitably. But no, the most dozy baby seagull remained on the original side. No one would slip a mere two out of three seagulls onto a neighbouring balcony, would they? Manual seagull shifting was obviously an "all or nothing" kind of activity.

It seemed to Rees that either the fledgling gulls would die when the afternoon sun moved around and directed its full force on the balconies or they would tough it out and remain there for weeks, turning his balcony into a tip. Neither prospect appealed. Something must be done. But what to do? The RSPCB didn't seem inclined to take direct action. The buck appeared to have stopped with the flat. Marian and his wife had made themselves scarce but Rees was pleased to find Colin standing shoulder to shoulder with him. Four against two, rather than four against one, seemed so much better odds. They began to prepare their campaign. Fortunately, a local had told Rees that for years baby seagulls had successfully fledged in the undergrowth across the road from the gardens, confirming a possibility that had occurred to Rees.

Now, you never know when you might be called upon to do some impromptu seagull moving in the face of maternal opposition, so it may be useful to itemise the common household equipment that can be moulded to the task. Oven gloves are good for the actual bird handling. A plastic cool box makes a good transport container and then a couple of medium-sized plastic trays come in useful for "bangers" to scare off the mother bird.

It being Rees's balcony, he had rather expected to be pencilled in to do the "heavy lifting", but no. Colin had watched a few key episodes of *Country File* and insisted that he knew a thing or two about bird handling and had taken on board key information such as "they'll be calm if it's dark"; hence, the cool box and lid. It was Colin, then, who bagged the first two chicks while Rees took the role of "rear gunner", the staccato chatter of the twin tea trays keeping the "fighter" at bay.

The first two chicks were placed in the undergrowth in an unexposed place as carefully as possible, under the watchful eye of the mother bird. There remained the problem of the dozy chick, which had not made "The Great Leap Forward". Well, Colin had the bit between his teeth by now and, moving like a panther, with the covering fire of the tea trays, shimmied over the balcony partition, boxed the last chick and took it to join its peers.

The day seemed even hotter or perhaps the adrenaline of the moment made it seem so. In any event, Rees felt sorry for the birds and took them down some water under the watchful eye of their circling mother.

There was no certainty as to how things turned out. The birds were still there that evening when the group returned from the pub, but by the next morning at least some were seen to be sheltering in more extensive cover.

The last word went to Rees's wife: 'If they'd been spiders, I'd have been more help.' Rees made a mental note to give her primacy, should there ever be foot-high spiders on the balcony, guarded by a ferocious mother.

Portage

Eileen was a Portage worker. Portage is the sort of service that everyone thinks should exist, but prefers someone else to pay for. Essentially, once a week, Portage workers visit houses containing a pre-school child with difficulties. They work with parents to help the child progress. Priorities are agreed, activities demonstrated, materials loaned and progress reviewed the following week.

The Portage service Eileen worked for had to "Obtain Client Feedback", "Review Client Satisfaction Ratings" and "Seek to Continuously Improve." Eileen was getting on a bit these days, had worked in the service for fifteen years and wasn't sure she had the capacity to improve much more. Secretly, she thought she might have been at her best about ten years ago, when her energy levels were at their peak. Overall ratings for the service were "satisfactory to good". However you did not have to "deep dive" to note, that those actually receiving the weekly visits almost universally rated the service as "excellent", while those who had received one or two interim visits during their year on the waiting list were much less impressed. Perhaps the obvious conclusion was that more Portage workers were required, though this did not seem apparent to the budget holders. It may be, though, that some readers (surely you are not one?) are feeling that there could be an efficiency issue to consider? Rather like care staff visiting old people, perhaps the visitors could be whipping around a few more families in what managers would regard as a blaze of ruthless efficiency?

Certainly, Eileen was not ruthlessly efficient. However, her inefficiency took the form of often working ten-hour days rather than seven-and-a-half-hour ones. It was expected that, during the hourly visits, time would be taken with parents to listen to their feelings about having a child with difficulties, and to try and ensure that relationships with medical and educational professionals remained positive. What was rather more "off piste" as far as the Portage manual was concerned were discussions about debt, threatening ex-partners and rows with friends or family. Though aware that these were potentially deep and murky waters, Eileen did tend to enter into some discussion and to try and suggest some positive options. She was aware that this was further over a boundary than she should, or indeed wanted to go, but this seemed more humane and less destructive to the relationship than advancing the view that "I'm here to help Ronnie and can't offer advice on your financial situation".

Eileen knocked on the door of a small flat.

A pity there's not a bit of garden for Kyle to play in, she thought.

'Hello Eileen,' said Chloe, opening the door invitingly. 'He's done ever so well with the bricks. Just come and have a look.'

She led Eileen into the living room where Kyle was rambling around in quite a free range sort of way. Chloe lifted him up and placed him at the table.

'Kyle, do the bricks......Do the bricks, Kyle.'

Kyle eyed the blocks in front of him rather suspiciously at first, but then, glancing at Chloe and Eileen, placed first one, then another on a third.

'Well done, Kyle; good boy,' said Chloe.

Kyle, seemingly satisfied with a job well done, climbed down and made off to leaf through a catalogue.

'That's really good,' said Eileen to a beaming Chloe, 'And how's he getting on with our other target, "Constructive Mark Making with a Felt Tip"?'

'Oh, I did try, Eileen, honestly I did, but he just holds them like a dagger and he stabbed them onto the paper and the ends got all squashed and we couldn't use them after two or three goes.'

'Never mind,' said Eileen. 'Maybe we can try him with a paintbrush; just a small one with stiff bristles, just to help him get started.'

'But won't that make a horrible mess?'

'Well, we'll be able to use paint that's easy to wash off and we can try it in the kitchen rather than in here where there's carpet.'

'Oh Eileen,' said Chloe, suddenly changing the subject, 'I met this bloke called Ryan in the supermarket and he seemed really nice and he asked me to go for a drink with him on Saturday and I might be able to get my sister to come over and look after Kyle; do you think I should go?'

'He's single, is he, this Ryan?' asked Eileen.

'Oh, he must be, mustn't he, or he wouldn't have asked me out...'

'Well, it might be an idea to check if you can.'

'Well, if he is, do you think I should go?'

'Well, you'd want to know,' said Eileen, sounding to herself like her own grandmother, 'That he liked you as a person and that you had things in common and everything, wouldn't you?'

And so the conversation continued for another few minutes until Eileen managed to haul it back around to Kyle...

'Well, you'll just have to make up your own mind, but make sure you have a good think first... Now let's get Kyle trying to do some painting...'

'Oh yes,' said Chloe. 'Just give me a minute, though; the kitchen isn't quite as tidy as it should be.' And off she went.

Thirty seconds later, she was back screaming.

'Eileen, Eileen, there's a rat in the kitchen! It's horrible! Oh, what can we do? It might bite Kyle.'

'Are you sure?' asked Eileen.

'Of course I'm sure. Urrrgh; it's horrible. You go and have a look; just go and see.'

Thinking this really was beyond the call of duty, Eileen advanced to the kitchen door.

'Don't let it in here; don't let it in here!' wailed Chloe.

Sure enough, as Eileen opened the door, a large brown blur shot across the floor and disappeared from view behind a cupboard. Eileen shut the door quickly.

'Did you see it? Was it still there?' asked Chloe.

'Yes,' said Eileen, rather shaken herself.

'Oh, what can we do?' asked Chloe. 'They carry diseases, you know. If it bit me or Kyle we could die or something.'

'Let's keep calm,' said Eileen, to herself as well as Chloe. 'We're in here and the rat's in there. I think we'll have to get a pest control man round.'

'But I haven't got any money to pay him,' said Chloe.

'Just let me do a bit of investigating,' said Eileen, taking out her mobile phone.

'We're lucky,' said Eileen some time later. 'The council still does rat extermination for free; mice no, wasps no, but rats yes. I explained you were a single parent with a little boy and they've made you a priority. There's a bloke in the area and he'll be round in an hour or two when he's finished his current job.'

'You're not going to go, are you, Eileen? You're not going to go and leave me alone with that rat?'

Eileen had, in fact, been due to return to the office to write up some six-monthly reviews, but she didn't seem to have much choice. She managed to use some of the time by getting Kyle to sit on the settee with her and to look at a picture book. She encouraged Chloe to do the same, but her mind was far too rat oriented for her to concentrate.

At last came the knock on the door.

'My name's Paul,' said the chap at the door, flashing some identification. 'I understand there's a rat on the premises.'

'It's in the kitchen,' said Chloe. 'It's horrible; it's really big and scary.'

Paul thrust open the door and boldly walked in.

'Don't worry,' he said. 'He's not going to come out while we're about. Now, where did you last see him?'

Eileen pointed to the relevant cupboard. Paul walked over.

'Yeah, there's a gap there big enough. If he's active and hungry, he might come out again if we're not here. Tell you what, you make me a cup of tea and take it in there and I'll set my traps. If it doesn't work, I'll have to use poison, but I don't like doing that with little ones in the house and he might die under cover and then there'd be a right pong.'

Chloe did as he said and some minutes later they were collected in the sitting room drinking tea when there was a snap of metal on metal.

'That's him,' said Paul, and he sprang up and marched off to investigate.

A few seconds later, he poked his head around the door.

'I know this is a bit distressing for you ladies, but you'd best come and have a look.'

The pair edged reluctantly into the kitchen and there in a small trap was an average-sized mouse.

'I set two kinds of trap, just in case,' said Paul.

'But we were sure it was a rat,' said Eileen.

'It's surprising how your eyes can deceive you when you're in the grip of strong emotions,' Paul answered philosophically. 'Now if you're lucky, there's just this one, but if you see any more, call me back or set some traps yourselves.'

'Oh,' said Chloe miserably. 'Eileen, you said we had to pay for mice and I haven't any money.'

Paul grunted as he completed some paperwork.

'Now ladies, you just have to sign here, to say I've completed the job.'

And there on the job description was written: "Successful extermination: one pygmy rat."

St Paul's

Rees received an email from his old school friend, Martin, suggesting that if he was ever in London they should meet up, together with another friend, Brian. Rees liked the idea, so a meeting was arranged. Rees had met Martin occasionally, but there had been no contact with Brian since leaving school some forty years before.

They were to meet one Saturday at 12pm, in a café in the city and, having time on his hands, Rees left his hotel at 9am, thinking he would take the opportunity to explore St Paul's Cathedral.

Despite baulking somewhat at the price, Rees pressed on with his small, but heavy suitcase. First, though, it had to be searched by a Muslim. Rees felt guilty about contemplating this at all. He knew that he should be pleased that a dedicated member of the security personnel was carrying out a precautionary, but necessary, impersonal search of visitors' bags for their mutual safety in this difficult age, rather than considering it to be ironic that a Muslim should be seeking to prevent an elderly white Christian from potentially blowing up a church no doubt festooned with memorials commemorating military defeats of the heathen.

The search was a thorough one and Rees had an irrational fear that the searcher had read his foolish mind and was consequently determined to leave no stone unturned and the interior of no shoe unexamined. He stopped short of tasting Rees's toothpaste to ensure the content was as described, but Rees felt it to be a close run thing.

Arriving in the cathedral, Rees began to think the considerable fee well spent. As well as the glories of the building itself, there were statues and tombs.

Here was a chap who had lashed the prow of a much larger French frigate to the back of his own and forced it into submission via a good pounding with his stern cannon, unfortunately being killed in the process.

Over there was a bloke who had visited a lot of prisons and, not liking what he saw, had forced through sensible and much-needed reform.

And now a doctor who was "always willing to take into account the opinions of others while sensibly never underestimating his own".

Rees had to admit that, taking a line through this kind of form, it was unlikely that there would be a marble statue of him for future generations to ponder. No, he was rather far from even gaining the sort of plaque "Raised by Public Subscription" or "Financed by his Family and Grateful Colleagues". No, he would be lucky to get a decent leaving card, and "reassuringly normal, an underrated quality" seemed the best he could do in terms of plaudits. Rees noted that the "big hitters", led by Nelson and Wellington, managed both a statue in the body of the cathedral and a tomb in the crypt.

Rees noticed that there were further areas to explore. In addition to the crypt, there were principally: The Whispering Gallery , The Stone Gallery and The Golden Gallery. Was he going to let a small, but heavy suitcase restrict his access to these? No, he was not. Sixty plus he might be, but surely he could carry it up a few hundred steps? Fiddling with his audio guide, Rees discovered that there were two hundred and fifty-nine steps up to The Whispering Gallery, a hundred and nineteen more to The Stone Gallery and a further hundred and fifty to The Golden Gallery.

So, off he went, up the dark and winding staircase. There was some kind of honour at stake here. He should not be overtaken except perhaps by an occasional unfettered person under thirty. Perhaps fortuitously for his health and well-being, he found himself behind a rather stout middle-aged French couple. After a few winds of the stair, they would pause to pant *"Mon Dieu, quel escalier!"* or something similar.

In the context of a dark and winding staircase, it is difficult to exude to the world at large the impression that "of course, I wouldn't want to pause here myself, but in the circumstances what other option is there?", but Rees did his best. Perhaps a bit too effectively, because, after an estimated one hundred and forty steps, the French couple edged into a narrow passing place and, with an :

'Apres vous, monsieur,' waved him on.

Unfortunately, the French family extended the courtesy to a number of others and so Rees now found himself "leading the peloton", having hit the front rather sooner than he would have liked, though feeling those behind were gaining only very limited benefit from reduced wind resistance.

He made it to the top, though those looking closely may have seen people at the other side looking puzzled as though wondering "is this The Whispering Gallery or the Puffing and Blowing Gallery"?

Naturally, under the circumstances, Rees decided that the depictions of the life of St Paul on the underside of the dome needed to be given lengthy consideration. He was also interested to learn from his audio guide that, when Sir Christopher Wren had thought he had better come up to check the builders weren't skimping on the mortar or drinking too much tea (or should that be ale?), he'd had himself winched up with the building supplies rather than braved the staircase.

However, The Stone and Golden Galleries still beckoned. Rigorous Rees and Pragmatic Rees began to argue.

'Both of these galleries are outside and give essentially similar views of London, one just being slightly higher,' said Pragmatic Rees.

'You should do them both,' said Rigorous Rees.

'Why?' asked Pragmatic Rees 'I won't really see anything different.'

'I believe the traditional retort is "because they're there",' answered Rigorous Rees.

'But that's a hundred and nineteen more steps versus two hundred and sixty-nine and for no practical purpose and all with a small but heavy suitcase,' replied Pragmatic Rees.

In the end, Pragmatic Rees prevailed and "only" a further one hundred and nineteen steps were climbed. Rees's stay at the top was relatively brief, as the rain was starting to set in, but the view of the river, the Tate and so on was still rewarding.

The descent was relatively plain sailing and, on reaching the ground floor, Rees, glancing at his watch, noted there were thirty minutes left before the meeting. He also noticed that somehow, in the process of his labours, the zip of his coat had unmoored itself and was stuck halfway up, with both the top and bottom part of the zip open.

How on earth has that happened? wondered Rees.

Some remediation was obviously necessary. He didn't want to meet Martin and Brian in a coat with a zip stuck in the middle and have to take it off by lifting the whole garment over his head; no indeed, he must sort this out now.

Handily, in front of him was a bare table on which he was able to lay the offending garment. Now he could get to grips with it properly. Surely a repair could be affected? He concentrated hard. It would move up easily enough, but then, down it would come, hit the road block and go no further.

'Patience; that's what's required,' muttered Rees, but, ten minutes later, the situation remained unchanged.

Perhaps if I move it all the way to the top, he thought, *it will either glide down freely or I'll somehow be able to disengage it from one side or the other.*

The difficulty when this plan failed was that he could no longer push his head through the small opening. It was impossible to put on the coat at all.

Sod, sod, sod, thought Rees, but restrained himself from verbal utterance owing to the sanctity of his surroundings.

A related thought occurred to Rees. *Would a small prayer do the trick?*

But he baulked at this. Surely God had other priorities, rather than helping the hapless put on their coats? Also, Heaven would be a poor sort of place if its denizens had no sense of humour. Perhaps those managing eternal salvation had a sort of "Pathetic Prayer of the Week Competition"? If so, Rees didn't want to be in contention.

Nor did he find the situation improved by the presence of the shades of Nelson and Wellington.

'What the devil's going on over there, Duke?'

'Damned if I know, Lord N; chap here seems unable to put on his own coat.'

'Limited Empire building material, what?'

'Not a candidate for the "Thin Red Line of Heroes", certainly.'

And so on.

Time moved on. Either he could arrive like some kind of Headless Horseman with his eyes spying out of the buttonholes of his coat or with his coat inexplicably over his arm in a thunderstorm. He chose the latter.

Fortunately, the café was situated in a block of several buildings with a first-floor overhang. He could, therefore, aim himself at the nearest corner rather than directly at the café door, in full view of his friends.

He chose the corner and dashed across, his case banging noisily on the cobbles, the architect having opted for aesthetic effect rather than thunderstorm practicalities.

Rees then sauntered along the covered perimeter of the building, trying to appear, as he reached the café door, like a man who had removed his perfectly practical, quality coat in good time, prior to making his entry.

In the end, it was all for nothing. The leopards had not changed their spots. There was scarcely any of the "wallet weighing" that Rees had feared, particularly given that Brian was a retired banker. Their dress was entirely informal. Rees had hardly got his feet under the table before Martin was ripping open his shirt to show his pacemaker scar and Brian's "coat" was one of those plastic affairs bought off a market stall when surprised by the weather.

Rees was relieved by the open camaraderie of his friends and forgot his disproportionate concern about his coat. Soon, the reminiscences and updates were in full swing. Let the Duke and Nelson think what they liked; Rees was enjoying himself.

The Scan

Rees's colleagues were mostly women. Just now, most of them were clustered around one of their number, peering at some sort of photo.

'Look,' said Lianne as he walked past. 'This is Kimberley's baby!'

Rees peered at the image. Through the static, he could just about make out a foetus. He knew that not a lot was expected of him in this situation and fortunately he had a few seconds to consider his response.

'Lovely,' he replied and, cunningly adding about twenty-eight weeks to the current date, he added, 'The due date is October, isn't it?'

'That's right,' said Kimberley. 'The twenty-fourth.'

Rees had done enough and soon he could move on. He was unsettled though; past memories kept intruding into his consciousness.

When Rees was nine, his mother got pregnant. Rees had had some idea about how babies were made and it had seemed to him that thirty-five was rather old to be participating in that kind of peculiar business.

The phrase "it is what it is" was not current in the sixties, but, as far as he could recollect, Rees reached a similar conclusion at the time and, being an analytical sort of boy, began to consider the practicalities. Where, for instance, was this baby going to sleep? His parents had a room; his sister had a room; he had a room. There were no others. For the first time, Rees decided that he was pleased that his sister had a substantially bigger room than his own. Surely there was an argument to be made there?

The pregnancy did not go smoothly and "bed rest" was ordered. This was not a concept with which Rees was familiar. But it did not seem very subtle. His mother went to bed and, well... rested.

She was visited by various colleagues from the National Coal Board (NCB) where she worked as a secretary. Rees was impressed by one in particular, Mr Hollins.

Mr Hollins had been a merchant seaman on an armed vessel in convoys during the war and, given the limited conversational possibilities when visiting the sick, had been unusually forthcoming in discussing this under Rees's probing.

No, he had not regarded himself as especially brave. If a Stuka was dive bombing you, surely the only sensible thing to do was to fire back?

Yes, he had been scared, as had everyone else. The Stukas were designed to make a horrible noise as they dived and this added to the general concern.

They had gained in confidence, though. The Stukas had tended to use straight lines of attack and needed to get fairly low. If you fired sufficiently ahead of them and maintained your aim, eventually they would fly through it, with the possibility of damage.

Yes, the flotilla had shot down a few. No, he had no idea whether he had contributed himself.

It was difficult to get Mr Hollins to return to this topic on future visits, but comments during another turned out to be even more worthwhile.

Rees's parents had been fortunate enough to have been offered the opportunity to buy a former NCB house on favourable terms, owing to a family history in the coal mining industry. House purchase would otherwise have been beyond their means. The house was on the fringe of the more affluent part of town and Rees consequently found himself substantially less well off than his friends. This was not generally referred to among the group, status depending more upon sporting capability and traditional qualities of character. There were some practical repercussions, though. Rees did not have a bike, whereas the others had glittering, geared examples. At times, the group would go out on bike rides. Sometimes Rees would run, getting a turn on someone else's bike occasionally. However, this was not really satisfactory and more often he did not go. One such example came to light during one of Mr Hollins's visits when he enquired why Rees wasn't out with his friends.

'What? You haven't got a bike?' he asked with some surprise.

He made no further comment for a few minutes and the conversation meandered around doings in the office. Then suddenly he said, 'I'm buying

Sarah a new bike for her birthday. You can have her old one, if that's okay with your parents.'

Rees couldn't believe it and stammered his enthusiastic thanks.

'Don't get your hopes up too much. It hasn't got any gears and it's a vivid pink.'

Rees said he didn't care what colour it was; he'd just be glad to have a bike.

Mr Hollins contemplated some more.

'Tell you what, give me a week and I'll paint it grey. It won't be all shiny or anything, but it won't be pink.'

And so, the grey girls' bike was delivered and out Rees went on it.

'What are you doing on a girls' bike?' sneered Jeffrey Brown, a fringe member of the group. 'And look, it hasn't even got gears.'

Matters hung in the balance, but two of Rees's closest friends intervened.

'Doesn't matter what kind of bike it is. He can come with us now.'

'Bet he could beat you on it, Brown, gears or no gears; what do you say?'

Brown was considerably chubbier than he would have liked to be. He was not daft and saw the snag immediately; if he won, so what? By his own admission, he had the much better bike – but if he lost…

'No, not worth it,' he replied. 'Come on or we'll be late.'

And there the matter rested.

Rees's mum was admitted to hospital a week or two before Christmas at something Rees heard

referred to as "around thirty-two weeks gestation".
Rees and his sister were not allowed to visit and so
his mind turned to practicalities.

Rees noticed his father seemed rather overwrought. *Would he be able to cook Christmas
dinner properly?*, Rees wondered. *Had all the
presents been bought?* And it seemed he was right
to be concerned. On a visit to town, his father
suddenly announced:

'I'm going to buy you each a book as part of
your Christmas present. Do you want it to be a
surprise or to choose it yourselves?'

The children decided a surprise would be best
and were sent elsewhere in the shop while the
purchases were made.

En route for home, a stop was made for petrol
and there was a considerable queue to pay. The
children were in the back of the car along with the
bag containing the books.

'Shall we just have a quick look?' wondered
Rees. His sister agreed and peeks were made and
the choices deemed suitable. The children thought
the bag had been replaced as it had been, but their
father was sharper-eyed than they thought.

'That bag has been moved and messed about with,'
he said. 'You've been looking in it, haven't you?'

Rees wondered about a stout denial, but his
younger sister's lip was already quivering, fraction-
ally ahead of an admission of wrongdoing.

'Right then, you can say goodbye to those
presents, because you won't be getting them.'

'What will you do with them?' asked his sister,
bursting into tears.

'I shall throw them in the bin,' said their father, with complete finality.

And on arriving home, so he did, in full view of the miscreants. Rees did notice, however, that the books were carefully wrapped in a plastic bag and placed right on top of the contents of the bin. His father went to get some lunch ready and Rees was left looking out of the window, feeling, not contrite, but very cross. Suddenly, further up the street, a dustbin van hove into view, its occupants emptying bins as they came up the street. Should he mention this to his father? if so, directly or more casually? No, he decided, he wouldn't. His father had said he was throwing them away and so he jolly well would. Rees watched in a kind of horrified fascination as the bin men took the bin down the drive and emptied it into the truck. Part of him began to regret saying nothing. Then, to his surprise, one of the dustbin men advanced up the path and knocked on the door. He wanted a "Christmas box". Rees deemed it sensible to remove himself as his father moved towards the door and it was from behind a bedroom curtain that he observed his father dash down the path and rummage in the back of the truck, with the aid of the bin men, who were evidently earning their "box".

Tact and common sense can be better developed in some nine-year-olds than many imagine and, a few minutes later, Rees ate his lunch without alluding to the matter at all.

The house had a phone. Its rental was paid by his father's employers, as it was sometimes necessary to contact him in an emergency. One evening, this phone rang. Rees and his sister were packed off to sleep at a neighbour's house, while their father went off to the hospital. He was a long time coming back and, when he did so, he explained that their mother had had twins, but that all three were very ill. The children asked if they could visit, but their father said no. He explained that the twins were likely to die and that the doctors thought it best for the children to stay away so that they did not become very attached. It is very difficult to recollect precise feelings over several decades. Rees could not remember what he had thought about the plight of the twins. Being older and more logical than his sister was, he did, though, have one immediate and intense concern. "All three are very ill and the twins might die..." What, then, of his mother? He enquired later when his sister was asleep.

'She's not very well either,' came the scary reply. 'We shall just have to wait and see.'

After a lapse of decades, Rees found it difficult to remember whether his anxiety centred mostly on love for his mother and personal concern for her or more self-centred concerns regarding who on earth would look after him if she died. Certainly both featured.

The twins did die and his mother didn't. They were referred to occasionally, but the intense feelings his parents must have experienced were kept largely to themselves and Rees's life continued much as before.

Rees revisited the event for the last time with his father, in the latter's old age. He had been shocked to find that twins had not even been suspected until after the first baby had been delivered. He glanced back up at the women in the office and thought of the scan. There was a lot to be said for progress sometimes, he thought.

Bear

In films, toys sometimes seem to come alive and have adventures while children are asleep. This is much rarer in real life. Most real toys need children to help them have adventures. Even teddy bears never talk and very, very rarely move independently. This is because of the huge effort they need to make in order to move themselves and because of the length of time it takes for them to regain their strength and energy afterwards.

You may be thinking by now that a teddy bear's life must be a pretty boring one if they can't talk and can hardly move. But that is because, as a human, you are thinking from a human point of view. In any case, "existence" is probably a better word than "life". Because life implies death and a teddy bear cannot die except by accident or long-term neglect. Human beings spend a long time eating, drinking, sleeping and, when grown up, having children and working. A teddy bear does none of these. Using very little energy, he has no need to eat or drink. He absorbs the energy he needs from the body heat of humans. (That is why, if you ever think your teddy has moved himself, you need to give him an extra-long cuddle.) Teddy bears spend their days thinking and considering and remembering. This is the reason bears are so very knowledgeable and wise.

The difficulty lies in communicating their wisdom and ideas to other species. As a matter of fact, they can do this most easily to cats. But cats are not great creatures for conversation and think they have little to learn. They already know that eating, lying somewhere warm and being stroked are among the nicest things in life.

Bears can also communicate with humans, but this is often hard. Bears specialise in transmitting general feelings of comfort and niceness and can do this under almost any circumstances. However, more complicated transmission of ideas needs a very specialised environment. Important factors include: quiet, plenty of time and a calm, peaceful mind on the part of the human concerned. This is the reason why so many "good ideas" seem to occur at bedtime or early in the morning. Bears can communicate most easily with children and old people. Ordinary adults often seem too busy to listen carefully enough.

Evelyn was staying at her grandparents' house with her parents and her little sister. She was having a good explore round, like a visiting princess in a strange castle. She ran into a vacant bedroom. There, sitting on an old Indian table, was a one-eyed threadbare teddy bear.

'What's that?' she asked her grandad, who had followed her in.

'Oh, that,' said her grandad. 'That's the teddy bear I had when I was a boy. He must have been there for ages.'

And indeed he had; getting on for five years, in fact. It was so long since he had had a cuddle that he had less than a day of teddy bear energy left. If no one cuddled him within that time, all his knowledge and wisdom would be lost and he would become a shell of his former self and be like any other toy. The humans, of course, did not realise this.

'Can he come in my bed tonight?' asked Evelyn.

I really do hope so, thought the old bear.

'I don't see why not, if you'd really like him to,' said Grandad'

The bear stared at the clock across the room. Twelve o'clock. He estimated he had about six hours of teddy bear energy left. Evelyn looked like a good girl, but also a lively one. Surely she wouldn't be in bed ready to go to sleep by six o'clock? It would be too late for him. He must reconcile himself to his doom.

'Why has he only got one eye?' asked Evelyn.

'Because when he was a young bear and I was a young boy, we used to play fight and he lost an eye when we were boxing.'

'Oh, you poor bear,' said Evelyn and picked him up for a comforting cuddle.

Now as we have said, a teddy bear needs very little energy and the bear felt the warmth of the cuddle flow right through him. He took on board enough warmth and energy from that short cuddle to last a whole week!

I'm going to be all right, he thought.

There was a lot of banging and clattering and shouting and laughing in the house that day and the bear enjoyed listening to these old sounds. Then, around seven o'clock, he heard splashing. He knew what was happening, as I expect you do.

Like most teddy bears, he was stoic, which means bravely accepting of his fate. But even stoic bears have their hopes and so did he.

I hope Evelyn doesn't forget about me, he thought.

In the children's bedroom, Evelyn was just getting towards the end of her second and last book, with only the definitely very last book to go.

'Granny, what about the teddy?' she asked suddenly.

'Your cuddly toys are all in your bed,' said Granny.

'No Granny,' said Evelyn. 'The other teddy.' and before her granny could stop her, she jumped down and ran along the landing to the other bedroom.

'There he is!' she shouted and picked up the old teddy.

'Yes, he looks as though he could do with a good cuddle,' said Granny, speaking the truth more than ever she knew.

And so it was that the teddy snuggled up to Evelyn all night and, by the morning, he had absorbed so much warmth that his energy reservoirs were brimming full.

He had done useful work during the night too. Like most teddy bears, he was very fond of picnics and he had helped Evelyn to dream about one. There had been Evelyn, her mummy and daddy, her sister, her granny and grandad and teddy himself. How many was that? How many plates would they need? How many cups? When all this had been sorted out, there had been all sorts of lovely things to eat in the picnic dream.

Now, though, it was time for the humans to get up. Teddy was left to have a bit longer in bed.

A little later, in toddled Evelyn's little sister, whom the bear had learnt was called Isobel. She was holding some car keys and teddy began to worry. He had been on many journeys in his long life and knew that these keys were needed to make the car go.

'Keys,' said Isobel to the world in general and, spotting the lock on the wardrobe door, she tried to push the keys into it. They fell down behind a waste bin where they were very hard to see. Isobel looked puzzled, but was distracted by the arrival of her mother.

'Come on, Isobel,' she said. 'We need to get you changed' and off the pair went.

The teddy bear could see disaster looming, but what could he do? nothing but worry at the moment.

Sure enough, towards the end of the day, the teddy bear began to hear cases being dragged downstairs and the sound of car doors and boots being opened and the general sounds of a family leaving. Evelyn, Isobel and their mummy and daddy thought they were going home.

Teddy bear winced as the fierce conversation he had anticipated began.

'Have you got the keys?'

'No, you had them.'

'You must have had them when you put the car seat in yesterday.'

'I'm sure I saw you with them in the bedroom.'

A frantic look round began. Evelyn's mummy and daddy had jobs to go to the next day and how could they do their jobs if they couldn't even get home?

A whole house search started. Teddy bear knew what he must do. Just worrying was no use; action was required. A good job he was full of energy after his all-night cuddle. As a test, he gave his left paw a good hard stare and concentrated with all his might. Yes! It quivered slightly. Teddy bear stopped straight away. He must keep his energy for the crucial moment.

The situation seemed to be getting even more heated. Apparently Evelyn's daddy had lost things before and Evelyn's mummy and granny seemed to think it would be helpful to remind him of this. Teddy bear felt sorry for Evelyn's daddy. After all, it wasn't his fault this time, was it? He hadn't lost the keys. Eventually, the door burst open.

'I don't know why you're even bothering to look in there,' said an angry voice. 'They can't be in there, can they?'

Evelyn, who was feeling a bit worried, ran over, picked up teddy bear and gave him a big cuddle. Now was the time! He made a huge effort to transfer his thoughts and instructions:

'Go to the wardrobe, Evelyn; go to the wardrobe.'

Evelyn was taking a few steps in the right direction when her granny intervened.

'Shall I just give the children a yoghurt and a drink while you keep looking for the keys?' she asked Evelyn's mum.

'Yog!' shouted Isobel enthusiastically.

Thought transference is a complex process and cannot win against the immediate prospect of yoghurt. Was all lost?

No! Just as Evelyn was about to stop and retrace her steps, teddy bear, using nearly all his energy, wriggled free and began to drop to the floor.

There wasn't a teddy bear in England that could have crawled across the floor from a static start to the bin. But this teddy had the momentum of the fall to help him and, giving a kind of parachutist's roll, he travelled a good metre closer to the bin. Would it be far enough?

Evelyn moved over to pick him up. She glanced past him and yes! She glimpsed the keys.

'Look, Mummy, are those the right keys?'

Her mother came over and gasped with delight.

'Yes they are, Evelyn; tremendous work,' said her mum gratefully. 'You've really saved the day; well done, Evelyn!'

And, of course, with the help of the teddy, she had.

Lightning Source UK Ltd.
Milton Keynes UK
UKHW010716050720
365992UK00003B/215